The Phoenix'

Unlocking the Secrets of Fire and Fate

Elara Quinn

Copyright © 2024 by Elara Quinn

All rights reserved. No part of this book may be used or reproduced in any form whatsoever without written permission except in the case of brief quotations in critical articles or reviews.

First Edition: October 2024

Table of Contents

Chapter 1 Whispers of Fire 1

Chapter 2 Veiled Pathways 13

Chapter 3 The Genie's Warning 27

Chapter 4 Shadows of the Past 40

Chapter 5 The Trials Begin 54

Chapter 6 Echoes of the Forgotten 66

Chapter 7 Symbols and Secrets 80

Chapter 8 Bound by Oath 93

Chapter 9 Unseen Forces 107

Chapter 10 The Flame's Price 120

Chapter 11 A Rift in Purpose 133

Chapter 12 Reflections of Resilience 144

Chapter 13 Scorched Histories 155

Chapter 14 Awakening the Fire 166

Chapter 15 The Heart of the Phoenix 177

Epilogue Ashes and Embers 187

Chapter 1
Whispers of Fire

The desert storm was relentless, hurling walls of sand at them in furious gusts that cut across the dunes. Each step was a fight against the wind's howl, and yet Amal pressed forward, her eyes fixed on the horizon. Her scarf flared behind her like a banner, flapping wildly as if it, too, refused to be contained.

"Amal, this is madness!" Tariq's shout barely cut through the roar. His face was half-hidden behind his raised arm, shielding himself from the sandstorm's assault, but his gaze never left her. "We need to turn back. This isn't worth—"

"Worth it?" She whipped her head around, a glint of fierce determination flashing in her eyes. "Tariq, do you know how long I've waited for this? How many ancient texts I've scoured, how many sleepless nights I've spent piecing this together? I'm not turning back because of a little sand."

"This isn't a 'little sand,'" Tariq grunted, his voice tense. He stumbled as his foot sank into the shifting ground, but he caught himself, glancing warily at the darkening sky above. "This storm is bad enough to bury us alive. A little humility wouldn't kill you."

Amal laughed, a sound nearly swallowed by the wind. "Humility? You want me to walk away from centuries of legend because of humility?" She took a step toward him, her voice lower, but every bit as fierce. "This could be the place, Tariq. The gateway to the Phoenix. We're close—I can feel it."

"Or we're close to being two bodies in the desert." He tightened his grip on the strap of his pack, shaking his head. "Legends are called legends for a reason, Amal. They're stories, embellished over time to make them unforgettable. I think you've read one too many."

"Then why did you come with me?" she shot back, her eyes narrowing. "You could have stayed in that village. Or better yet, in that safe, quiet life you seem so content with."

"Someone had to come along to keep you from getting yourself killed," Tariq retorted, a mix of irritation and worry lacing his tone. "I came because you can't be reasoned with once you get an idea in that stubborn head of yours. You think you're invincible."

She sighed, her expression softening—only slightly. "It's not about being invincible, Tariq. It's about finding something worth risking everything for. Look around." She gestured at the endless, shifting sands, her voice taking on a reverent tone. "Somewhere out here, hidden by time and dust, is something that could change everything. Knowledge that goes beyond what we understand—power that could transform the world."

Tariq frowned, his gaze darting between her and the desolate landscape. "Or destroy it," he murmured, almost to himself. "You talk like you know what you're looking for, like you can control it. But what if the Phoenix isn't a gift? What if it's a warning?"

She paused, and for a brief moment, the weight of his words seemed to reach her. But then she shook her head, dismissing the thought as quickly as it had come. "That's the problem with you, Tariq. You're always waiting for the worst to happen. But what if—for once—you believed in the best? Believed that something incredible was just within reach?"

A long silence stretched between them, punctuated only by the storm's raging fury. Tariq exhaled slowly, a trace of doubt lingering in his eyes, but then he met her gaze, searching for a hint of doubt, a sign that she wasn't as sure as she claimed.

"Amal…what if this isn't the right way?" he said softly, his tone almost pleading. "What if there are things we're not supposed to find?"

She shook her head, her jaw set. "There is no 'right way,' Tariq. There's only the way forward."

He sighed, resigned. "So, what now?"

"We keep going," she replied, her tone firm. "The map—those symbols—I didn't misinterpret them. The gateway is near, I know it. The legends all point here."

"Legends." He shook his head, a mix of exasperation and reluctant admiration in his voice. "You've built your whole life around things no one's even proven exist."

"Sometimes, Tariq, legends are all we have left to guide us," she replied, her voice softening, almost wistful. She looked out over the dunes, a hint of something vulnerable beneath her defiance.

"And I'd rather follow them into the unknown than stay in a world that's content to let mysteries fade into dust."

They stood there, side by side, both silent, staring into the desert's vast, unforgiving expanse. The wind screamed around them, filling the air with a blinding fury, but Amal's gaze was unwavering. Tariq, feeling a mix of dread and loyalty, took a deep breath.

"Fine," he said at last, his voice barely audible over the storm. "But don't expect me to dig us out when this ends badly."

She turned to him, a triumphant glint in her eyes, and managed a smile despite the storm's biting cold. "Wouldn't dream of it."

And with that, she pressed onward, her every step a declaration of her resolve. Behind her, Tariq followed, every nerve in his body screaming at him to turn back. But he stayed close, driven by the unspoken promise that he would see this through, come what may.

As the storm raged around them, the first whispers of ancient power seemed to drift through the air, filling the space between them with the unspoken promise of secrets and shadows waiting to be uncovered.

The wind was a living thing, tearing at their clothes, clawing at their faces as if to push them back the way they'd come. Tariq trudged forward behind Amal, each step dragging as sand pooled around his feet, swallowing his boots with every movement. His face, half-hidden beneath a scarf, was twisted with worry, the intensity in his eyes matching the storm's fury.

"Tariq, are you keeping up?" Amal called over her shoulder, barely pausing as she looked back at him, her expression challenging. "I thought you said you'd stay with me through this."

He bit back a reply, fighting the urge to let his frustration slip. "I did say that. But I didn't expect this," he shouted, his voice rough as the wind swallowed half his words. "There's loyalty, Amal. And then there's recklessness."

"You think this is reckless?" She spun to face him, eyes flashing with a mixture of disbelief and amusement. "This is the desert's greeting, Tariq. Nothing more. People have faced worse."

"Oh, really? Worse?" he replied, raising an eyebrow despite the sand pelting his face. "So you think the desert's just testing us? Welcoming us into the fold?"

"Something like that," she replied, smiling. "You'll see. This place—these sands—they're like guardians. They'll push us, test us, but if we're strong enough, they'll let us pass."

He scoffed, shaking his head. "You talk about it like it's some sacred ritual. These aren't 'guardians,' Amal. It's just a storm, a storm that could kill us if we're not careful."

She tilted her head, eyes glinting with that familiar, unwavering confidence. "That's why you're here, isn't it? To be careful for me?"

Tariq's jaw tightened. "I'm here because I promised our family I'd look after you. Because someone has to think about what might happen if you push too far."

Amal's face softened, just a little. "Tariq, I appreciate it. Truly, I do. But I know what I'm doing."

"And what is that, exactly?" he challenged, not backing down. "What are you really looking for out here? Because it seems to me you're chasing shadows, stories."

"Stories?" She took a step closer, her voice quieter but intense. "These aren't just stories, Tariq. They're truths waiting to be uncovered, pieces of a world we've forgotten. You know that, don't you?"

"Maybe," he replied, hesitant. "But some things are forgotten for a reason."

She shook her head. "If we only ever accepted what we knew for certain, we'd have nothing. Nothing but what's in front of us, nothing but what's been handed down. I don't want that, Tariq. I can't live like that."

He sighed, glancing away, feeling the weight of her words. "I get it, Amal. I do. But why does it have to be you who digs up these truths? Why do you have to be the one risking your life for it?"

"Because I'm the one who cares enough to go after it," she answered simply, her gaze fierce. "Because I believe there's something out here that could change everything."

"And what if you're wrong?" he asked, his voice softer, almost vulnerable. "What if there's nothing here but ruins and legends that mean nothing?"

Her gaze didn't waver. "Then I'll know I tried. That's more than most people will ever say."

Tariq looked down, adjusting the strap of his pack to avoid her piercing stare. "And what am I supposed to do if it comes to that? If this all turns out to be... empty?"

She put a hand on his shoulder, forcing him to look at her. "Then we go home. Together. But we'll go back knowing we didn't let fear or doubt stop us."

There was a long silence as they held each other's gaze, the wind whipping around them, relentless as ever. Tariq felt his resolve shake, felt himself giving in to that fierce light in her eyes, the one that had pulled him into this journey despite his every instinct.

"You're impossible, you know that?" he muttered, though there was a reluctant smile tugging at his lips.

She grinned, the sandstorm forgotten in her eyes. "That's why you love me."

He shook his head, laughing despite himself. "Yeah. Love, or sheer exasperation. I'm not sure which."

"Both, I'd hope," she teased, nudging him forward. "Come on, let's go. The storm's letting up, see?"

He glanced around skeptically, watching as the wall of sand softened, revealing a clearer view of the horizon ahead. "And if it picks up again?"

"Then we take cover. But until then…" She took off, climbing the nearest dune with an agility that defied the harsh conditions. "There's something up ahead, I know it."

He watched her, torn between admiration and exasperation, before trudging up after her. "You're going to be the death of me, Amal. One day, I'm telling you."

She looked back at him, smirking. "Not today, Tariq. Not today."

And with that, she was off again, pushing through the sand, her steps unyielding, relentless, leaving him with no choice but to follow.

The wind had finally relented, settling to a restless murmur as they climbed the last dune. Below them, half-buried by centuries of sand, lay the remains of an ancient structure, its worn stones jutting out like the broken bones of some colossal creature. Even from a distance, Tariq felt the weight of the place pressing down on them, an echo of something that had long refused to die.

"There it is," Amal breathed, her voice barely above a whisper, yet charged with a thrill that made the hair on the back of Tariq's neck stand up.

"You don't even know what 'it' is," he replied, his tone a mixture of skepticism and caution. But despite himself, he couldn't look away. The structure was unlike anything he'd seen—part temple, part ruin, with markings etched into the stone that seemed to pulse faintly under the desert sun.

Amal descended the dune, her steps quick and sure as if pulled by an invisible thread. She knelt at the base of the structure, hands brushing the sand away to reveal faint carvings beneath. The intricate symbols seemed to twist and shimmer, catching the light in ways that defied logic. Tariq followed her, albeit more slowly, his gaze darting around as if expecting something to leap out from the shadows.

"Look at this…" Amal murmured, her voice filled with awe as her fingers traced the carvings. "These symbols… they're unlike anything I've studied. Ancient… older than the oldest records we have."

Tariq frowned, crouching beside her but keeping his distance from the stone. "It doesn't look welcoming," he said quietly, noticing how some of the symbols seemed to form jagged lines, almost like warning signs.

"Of course, it's not welcoming. It wasn't meant for just anyone," she replied, eyes fixed on the markings. "This… this is a gateway. I can feel it. Something powerful is buried here."

"Or something dangerous," Tariq muttered, his voice tense. His hand hovered over one of the symbols, an angular shape carved deeply into the stone. "Look at these lines. They're not just decorative, Amal. They're warnings."

She scoffed, brushing aside his caution. "Warnings? To whom, exactly? The people who built this place knew what they were doing. They wanted to protect something—something they valued enough to hide away. And we're the ones finally unearthing it."

"Or maybe we're the ones ignoring every obvious sign to turn back," he replied, a note of frustration in his tone. "Sometimes things are hidden for a reason, Amal. You said it yourself—this place is old. Too old for us to understand what we're messing with."

She looked up at him, eyes fierce with determination. "If we turn back every time we're afraid of something we don't understand, we'd never learn anything, Tariq. This isn't about playing it safe—it's about discovery. About pushing beyond what's comfortable."

Tariq sighed, glancing back at the open desert behind them, a vast expanse that suddenly seemed more welcoming than the mystery in front of them. "I just don't like how this feels. There's… something wrong here, Amal. Can't you feel it?"

"Feel what? That we're close to something remarkable? That we're about to uncover something that's been buried for centuries?" Her fingers continued tracing the lines, reverent, almost obsessive. "Because that's exactly what I feel, Tariq. And I'm not going to let fear stop me."

He watched her, a sense of unease gnawing at him as she uncovered more of the symbols. They were starting to form patterns now, shapes that looked familiar yet unsettling. Among them, he noticed a series of spirals encircling a central flame—a symbol he recognized from some of the older texts Amal had poured over.

"That looks like the Phoenix," he said, his voice barely above a whisper.

Her eyes brightened, following his gaze. "Yes… yes, it does." She brushed more sand away, uncovering a larger section of the carving. The figure of the Phoenix became clearer—a bird with wings spread wide, its feathers curling into flames that wrapped around the structure in intricate detail.

"Do you realize what this means, Tariq?" she said, her voice hushed with excitement. "We're on the right path. This… this could be the gateway to the Phoenix's power."

Tariq felt a chill creep down his spine, despite the heat. "Or a gateway to something else. Look at the edges," he said, pointing to the jagged lines that framed the Phoenix. They looked less like decoration and more like barriers, as though meant to keep something contained.

Amal shook her head, undeterred. "Symbols can be interpreted in a thousand ways. What you see as a barrier, I see as a boundary—one that we're meant to cross. There's nothing to fear here but our own hesitations."

"And what if that hesitation is the only thing keeping us safe?" Tariq's voice was tense, filled with a worry he couldn't shake. "Amal, listen to me. Just because something's hidden doesn't mean it's meant to be found."

She paused, finally looking up from the carvings to meet his gaze. "Tariq, I didn't come all this way, face all of this, just to stop now. These symbols, this structure… they're proof that we're onto something extraordinary. You don't have to understand it. Just trust me."

He sighed, rubbing a hand over his face, glancing back at the carvings one last time. "I trust you, Amal. I just don't trust… this."

She smiled, a spark of gratitude in her eyes, and returned to uncovering the rest of the markings, every brush of sand revealing another piece of the mystery. Tariq stood back, watching her, the weight of unease settling in his chest. The Phoenix symbol loomed over them, its fierce gaze seeming to pierce through the stone, as if warning them to proceed carefully—or not at all.

As Amal worked, muttering softly about ancient power and hidden knowledge, Tariq felt a sense of dread deepen. For every layer she unearthed, he sensed the cost growing, unseen and intangible, but unmistakably there.

In the silence that followed, he looked back at the open desert, wondering if this was their last chance to turn away.

Chapter 2
Veiled Pathways

The chamber seemed to hum with energy as Amal and Tariq stepped deeper inside, their torches flickering in the unsettling stillness. The air was thick with the weight of secrets long kept, and though they had already passed through rooms filled with forgotten artifacts and ancient carvings, nothing had prepared them for what lay before them now.

Amal's breath caught in her throat as her eyes fixed on the grand mural ahead. The wall stretched from floor to ceiling, dominating the room with its sheer size and intensity. At its center was the image of a phoenix, its wings ablaze with fire that seemed to pulse in the dim torchlight. The creature was majestic and terrible all at once, its eyes burning with life and death, its feathers shimmering with a heat that Amal could almost feel. Surrounding the phoenix were symbols—intricate, swirling, layered in ways that made them hard to discern from one another. Life and death, creation and destruction, all woven together in a pattern so complex it seemed to defy comprehension.

Amal took an involuntary step forward, her torch lowering as her gaze locked onto the mural. Her fingers itched to reach out, to trace the lines of the phoenix's wings, to understand. The breathlessness she felt wasn't just awe—it was a connection, a pull. This mural wasn't like the others. It felt alive, as though the flames on the bird's wings might leap from the wall at any moment.

"This is it," she whispered, more to herself than to Tariq. "This is what we were meant to find."

Tariq moved cautiously beside her, his own torch casting long, wavering shadows that seemed to shift unnervingly with every flicker of light. His gaze flickered between the mural and Amal, unease tightening his gut. The silence in the room was almost suffocating, broken only by the faint crackling of their torches.

"What is this place?" Tariq asked, his voice low, almost reverent, but heavy with unease. He couldn't tear his eyes away from the phoenix, and something about it—about the whole chamber—felt wrong to him, as though they were intruding in a place that had been sealed off for a reason.

Amal didn't answer at first. Her hand hovered near the mural, her eyes wide, captivated by the intricate details. "It's a story," she said softly, her voice carrying the awe that had overtaken her. "A story of life, death… and rebirth."

Tariq's brow furrowed. "Rebirth?" He stepped closer to the mural, his eyes catching on the symbols surrounding the phoenix. There was something unnerving in the way life and death were depicted, as if the line between the two was fragile—blurred. His instincts screamed at him that this wasn't just some ancient artwork. This was a warning.

Behind them, a figure that had been silent for too long shifted, the soft sound of cloth moving against stone. The genie, who had trailed them silently through the corridors of the lost city, finally spoke, his voice a low murmur that seemed to echo in the vast chamber.

"This place…" the genie said, his tone unreadable but laced with tension. "It was not meant to be found."

Amal turned, blinking as if snapped out of a trance. "What do you mean?"

The genie stepped closer, his tall figure casting a shadow over the mural. His expression was unreadable, but there was a tightness in his posture, a wariness that had not been there before. "The phoenix is a symbol of power, of life and death intertwined. But it is also a guardian. A keeper of balance." He paused, his dark eyes narrowing as they swept over the mural. "It was never meant for mortal eyes."

Tariq's hand instinctively moved to the hilt of his blade. The genie's words, coupled with his unease, only deepened the sense that they were standing on dangerous ground. "If it wasn't meant to be found, why is it here? Why leave something like this behind?"

The genie's gaze slid to Tariq, and for the briefest moment, there was something almost like pity in his eyes. "Because the past does not always stay buried."

Amal's curiosity flared again, pushing aside the growing tension in the room. "This phoenix," she said, turning back to the mural, "is more than just a symbol, isn't it? It's… connected to something real. Something powerful."

The genie didn't respond immediately, his gaze fixed on the flames depicted in the mural, as though he were remembering something long lost. "The phoenix is a conduit," he said at last, his voice quieter now. "It is life and death. To awaken it is to awaken forces that cannot be easily controlled."

Amal's heart skipped a beat. This was it. This was what she had been searching for. Not just relics of a forgotten past, but something more—something that pulsed with ancient power, with knowledge beyond anything they could comprehend. "Then we have to understand it," she said, a fire igniting in her own voice now. "If we can unlock what's hidden here, we could change everything."

Tariq stepped forward, his expression hard. "And what if unlocking it does more than change things? What if it destroys them?"

Amal turned to face him, her eyes bright with the intensity of her belief. "We've come this far. We can't turn back now, Tariq. This—this is why we're here."

Tariq held her gaze, but his unease remained. He couldn't deny the pull of the place, the way it seemed to call to them. But something about the mural, about the way the genie spoke of it, filled him with dread. "Amal, this isn't just about discovery anymore. It's about survival."

Amal smiled, though there was a sharp edge to it. "Survival has always been part of the journey. We knew the risks when we started."

The genie's voice cut through the tension like a blade. "Be careful, Amal. Not all journeys end in triumph."

But Amal had already turned back to the mural, her mind racing with possibilities. This wasn't the end of their search—it was only the beginning. And the phoenix, with its wings of flame, was the key to unlocking a power beyond their wildest dreams.

Amal's fingers traced each line of the carvings, feeling the delicate ridges and curves as though they could reveal something more to her than the mere texture of ancient stone. The torchlight flickered, casting shadows that made the inscriptions seem alive, writhing like coiling flames beneath her touch. Her eyes gleamed with excitement, the same glint that always appeared when she sensed discovery close at hand. Here, hidden under layers of stone and silence, lay the first hint of a puzzle older than any known civilization.

She leaned in closer, her breath catching as she began to read the words aloud, her voice reverberating softly in the chamber. *"He who solves the puzzle of life and flame shall inherit the wings of rebirth. Beware, for in light lies shadow, and in fire, the breath of death."*

Tariq watched her, his own heart sinking with each word she spoke. The inscriptions felt like warnings, woven with a sense of foreboding that seeped into his bones. But Amal—she saw only possibilities.

"Amal…" he began, a cautious edge in his tone, but she hardly seemed to hear him.

"This is it," she murmured, her fingers skimming over the symbols. "It's a riddle. A test left behind by whoever built this place. It's designed to keep the secrets of the phoenix hidden, to ensure only those worthy of its power can awaken it."

"Worthy?" Tariq echoed, incredulity and concern mingling in his voice. "Doesn't it strike you as strange that a test like this would be left out in the open, just waiting for someone to stumble across it?"

Amal looked up, her eyes alight with determination. "This wasn't meant for just anyone, Tariq. The city itself was hidden for centuries. Only those who would seek it out, who would have the will and courage to uncover it, could even reach this point." Her voice softened, almost reverent. "It's a safeguard, yes, but it's also an invitation."

He shook his head, his unease deepening. "Or a trap."

She ignored him, studying the lines of text again, piecing together the meaning hidden in each word. "Life and flame," she muttered, her brow furrowed in thought. "If it's a puzzle, then there must be a way to solve it. The phoenix represents rebirth through destruction—flame as both a creator and a destroyer."

Tariq took a step back, folding his arms as he watched her. "And what happens if you get it wrong? You don't know what kind of power you're dealing with here, Amal. This isn't some relic in a museum."

She glanced at him, irritation flickering across her features. "That's precisely why we have to solve it carefully. This could be the discovery of a lifetime—knowledge, power, maybe even something that changes everything we thought we knew."

Her fingers moved from the symbols to a series of smaller carvings just below them, depicting scenes of a phoenix rising from ash, surrounded by figures who looked both awed and terrified. Some figures reached for the phoenix, while others seemed to flee from it, their faces twisted in horror.

"Look here," she said, pointing to the figures. "This isn't just a story of rebirth. It's about balance. Those who approach the phoenix must understand both the creation and the destruction it embodies."

Tariq frowned, his gaze lingering on the images. "What if that's the real test, Amal? Not just understanding the phoenix, but knowing when to leave its secrets alone."

She shook her head, undeterred. "There's a way forward, Tariq. We just have to decipher it."

He sighed, feeling the weight of responsibility settle on his shoulders. Amal's excitement was infectious, yes, but it blinded her to the dangers lurking beneath the surface. And as much as he wanted to believe in the thrill of discovery, he couldn't shake the feeling that this place—this mural and its whispered secrets—held dangers they weren't meant to unearth.

"Let's think this through," he said, trying to keep his tone steady, reasonable. "If this is a test, we have to be certain we understand every part of it. One wrong move, and—"

"Then we go slowly," she cut in, her gaze intense but calm. "We study each symbol, each word, until we know exactly what's expected. The puzzle isn't here to frighten us off; it's here to make sure we're ready. That we truly understand what we're stepping into."

The genie, silent and watchful as ever, moved forward then, his eyes dark and unreadable as he regarded the carvings. "The puzzle is a gate," he said, his voice low and measured. "And a gate is a threshold—a boundary between what is known and what should remain unknown. Are you prepared to cross that?"

Amal looked at him, unflinching. "Yes. If it means uncovering the truth, then yes."

The genie's gaze didn't waver. "Truth is not the same as knowledge, nor is power the same as wisdom. The puzzle may reveal more than you wish to know."

Tariq's jaw clenched, frustration mounting. "Do you hear yourself, Amal? Even the genie is warning us. We're walking into something we might not survive."

Amal's expression softened, but her resolve remained unshaken. "I hear you, Tariq. But the truth is, I can't turn back now. This is what we've both been searching for—an answer to what's been hidden for so long. I need to see it through."

Tariq looked from her to the mural, his instincts still prickling with unease. The carvings glowed faintly under their torchlight, the phoenix seeming to shift in the shadows, its wings poised to rise in a blaze of fire and rebirth. As much as he feared what lay ahead, he knew he wouldn't abandon her, even if it meant stepping into a puzzle meant to guard secrets that could reshape their world.

"All right," he said finally, his voice low and resigned. "But we move carefully. We test every part of this, and if anything feels wrong, we pull back."

A smile flickered on Amal's lips, fleeting but grateful. "Deal. We do this together."

She turned back to the mural, determination burning bright as she prepared to confront the puzzle of life and flame, one careful step at a time. And though the shadows in the chamber seemed to deepen, as if the city itself was holding its breath, they pressed on, willing to confront whatever lay beyond the ancient carvings and hidden riddles of the phoenix.

The flames of their torches flickered uncertainly, casting long, twisting shadows across the stone chamber. The ancient carvings seemed to shift and warp in the low light, their once-clear meanings now shrouded in an ominous haze. Amal had grown quiet, her fingers still brushing over the delicate inscriptions, her mind working through the layers of meaning. The puzzle was deeper than it first appeared—more than just a test of intellect. Something far more dangerous lurked beneath its riddles.

Tariq stood several paces back, his arms crossed tightly, his body tense. He had been watching her for what felt like hours, the gnawing sense of dread only growing with each minute. The symbols, the warnings woven into every line of the puzzle—it was too much. He couldn't shake the feeling that they were standing at the edge of something far darker than either of them had imagined.

"We need to stop," Tariq said finally, his voice breaking the thick silence. His words were sharp, insistent, cutting through the air like a blade. "Amal, we don't know what we're dealing with here."

Amal didn't look up from the mural. "We know enough," she murmured, her tone distant, as if her mind was already elsewhere, deep in the labyrinth of the puzzle.

Tariq stepped closer, frustration bubbling to the surface. "No, we don't. You've heard the stories—the legends of the phoenix, the guardians of this place. This isn't just about knowledge, Amal. It's about something bigger. Something... darker."

She paused, her hand hovering just above the carving. Slowly, she turned to face him, her brow furrowed with irritation. "The stories are warnings meant to keep people away. Fear, Tariq— that's how secrets like this stay buried. If everyone gave in to doubt, to legends and old wives' tales, we wouldn't know anything about the past."

He took a breath, trying to steady himself, but the weight of his unease pressed down harder. "This isn't some relic in a museum. This is a city buried for a reason. A place filled with symbols of life and death, of powers we don't understand. The puzzle isn't here to test us—it's here to keep us from going any further."

Amal shook her head, her eyes narrowing in defiance. "Or it's here to challenge us, to make sure we're worthy of whatever knowledge lies ahead. You've always been the one to doubt, Tariq, but look around—this is what we've spent years searching for. If we don't take the risk now, we'll never know what could've been."

He clenched his fists, his voice growing quieter but no less intense. "And what if it's not knowledge waiting for us? What if it's something that was meant to stay buried? You keep pushing forward like this is just another archaeological dig, but it's not. There are forces at work here we can't begin to understand."

Amal's lips pressed into a thin line, her eyes filled with the same stubborn determination that had always driven her. "That's exactly why we *have* to understand it. If we don't, someone else will. And who knows what they'll do with the knowledge hidden here? We can't afford to turn back now, Tariq."

Her words hung in the air between them, filled with the weight of her conviction. But in the silence that followed, something else lingered—a shadow of doubt, of fear, gnawing at the edges of both their minds.

The genie stood at the far side of the chamber, his tall figure cloaked in shadow, watching them with a steady, unreadable gaze. His silence had been unnerving, but now it seemed deliberate, as if he were waiting for the inevitable.

Tariq's gaze flicked toward the genie, frustration flashing in his eyes. "You've been quiet long enough. What do you know about this place? You've been here before—what are you not telling us?"

The genie's dark eyes shifted, and for a moment, there was a flicker of something—perhaps unease, or perhaps something deeper—buried in his expression. He didn't respond right away, as though weighing his words carefully before speaking.

"This place," the genie said finally, his voice low and measured, "was not meant for mortals to unearth. It is older than any of your histories, older than the legends themselves. The phoenix is not just a symbol of rebirth—it is a force that balances life and death, creation and destruction. To awaken it is to upset that balance."

Amal turned toward him, her voice sharp with frustration. "You've been saying the same thing since we arrived. But you won't tell us why. What is the puzzle guarding? What happens if we solve it?"

The genie's gaze didn't waver, but there was a flicker of tension in his jaw. "The puzzle is not simply a key to knowledge. It is a test of your understanding of the forces that shape the world. Solve it, and you may unlock power—yes. But that power comes at a cost. Life and death are intertwined here, and one cannot exist without the other."

Tariq shook his head, his frustration mounting. "And what if the cost is too great? What if solving it awakens something that can't be controlled?"

Amal's eyes were filled with the fire of determination, but for the first time, there was a flicker of uncertainty. She glanced back at the mural, at the phoenix with its wings ablaze, surrounded by the figures of those who sought its power—some in awe, others in fear. She hesitated, her hand lowering from the carvings, her thoughts clouded with the weight of Tariq's words and the genie's cryptic warnings.

"We don't know what happens," she admitted quietly, almost to herself. "But we're here now, and we've come too far to turn back."

Tariq stared at her, his chest tightening with frustration and a growing sense of helplessness. He wanted to pull her back, to shake her free of the obsession that had taken hold. But he knew Amal—he knew her better than anyone. Once she had set her mind on something, there was no stopping her.

And so, doubt crept in, weaving its way between them like a shadow. Amal was standing on the edge of something far more dangerous than either of them could have imagined, and no amount of caution or warning seemed enough to hold her back.

The genie's gaze remained fixed on Amal, his silence heavy with unspoken truths. And though Tariq's heart told him to flee, he knew he would follow her into the depths of whatever this puzzle was, even if it led them into darkness.

Chapter 3
The Genie's Warning

The air inside the ancient corridor was thick and cold, each step Amal and Tariq took echoing down the stone passage. Strange shadows danced along the walls, shifting with the faint light that filtered through cracks in the ceiling. Tariq's grip tightened on his pack, his eyes darting around, sensing something… or someone watching.

"Amal," he whispered, his voice low but edged with tension. "Doesn't this place feel… off?"

Amal paused, her hand brushing against a faint carving on the wall, her gaze intent. "It feels… ancient. Like it's been waiting."

"Waiting for what?" he muttered, his eyes narrowing.

"Perhaps… waiting for us."

A voice, deep and resonant, slipped out of the shadows, startling them both. Amal turned sharply, eyes widening as a figure emerged from a dark alcove. Tall and imposing, the man was cloaked in layers of dark, shifting fabric that seemed to meld with the shadows. His face, half-lit, bore an expression of amusement tempered by something unreadable—a wisdom beyond time.

"Who are you?" Tariq demanded, instinctively stepping in front of Amal.

The figure tilted his head, a slow smile spreading across his face. "A guardian. A guide. I am many things… and yet, none."

"Very helpful," Tariq replied, his voice thick with distrust. "So which is it? Guardian or guide?"

"Neither would satisfy your curiosity, I'm afraid." The man's voice was a murmur that seemed to echo around them, yet he barely moved his lips. His gaze settled on Amal, dark eyes gleaming with a hint of recognition. "You've come a long way, seeker. Farther than most."

Amal stepped forward, undeterred. "You know who I am?"

He inclined his head slightly. "I know what drives you. The Phoenix, yes? The firebird that burns and rises anew. Its call echoes within you, even if you don't yet understand why."

Her eyes lit up, curiosity sparking like a flame. "Then you know where it is. The gateway. How to reach it."

The man smiled, but there was no warmth in it. "Knowledge is a heavy burden, child. Are you sure you wish to bear it?"

"More sure than anything," she replied, her voice steady. "If you know the way, tell me."

Tariq scoffed, crossing his arms. "And we're just supposed to trust you? A stranger lurking in the shadows?"

The man's gaze shifted to Tariq, his expression inscrutable. "Trust is an illusion. A flicker in the darkness, like a candle in a storm. I am here, not to be trusted, but to fulfill my purpose."

"And what purpose is that?" Tariq challenged, his posture rigid.

"To observe," the man replied simply. "To witness those who seek the Phoenix and judge whether they are… worthy."

Amal's eyes narrowed, searching his face. "Worthy of what?"

"Of the knowledge, the power, the curse… the gift." His voice lingered on each word, as though each held a different, layered meaning. "The Phoenix does not reveal itself to just anyone."

"So you're here to judge us?" Tariq's tone was incredulous. "Based on what? Our willingness to walk into some ancient death trap?"

The man's gaze was steady, unblinking. "Based on what lies within you. Fear, resolve, curiosity… these things will reveal themselves in time."

Amal tilted her head, a glint of curiosity in her eyes. "And who are you to judge us? What's your role in all of this?"

The man smiled faintly, but his eyes were cold. "I am bound, seeker. Bound to this place, to its secrets, to its whispers. You might call me a… keeper of the threshold."

Tariq snorted, folding his arms tighter. "So a glorified gatekeeper?"

"If that is how you wish to see it," the man replied, unperturbed. "But I am far older than any gate. I was here when this place was forged, when its secrets were sealed."

Amal took another step forward, her voice lowering. "Then tell me this—does the Phoenix still exist? Or are we following a trail of ashes?"

The man's gaze darkened, a flicker of something unreadable crossing his face. "The Phoenix exists, seeker. But what it is, and what you imagine it to be, are two very different things."

"Then tell me what it is," she pressed, her tone both eager and demanding.

The man shook his head slowly, as if speaking to a stubborn child. "That is not my role. The Phoenix reveals itself to those who earn its sight, not to those who demand it."

Tariq stepped forward, his voice thick with frustration. "So all this talk and no real answers. You're here to 'judge,' to 'observe,' but not to help?"

"Help…" the man murmured, his voice drifting like smoke. "Help is a mortal notion. I am not here to help or hinder. I am here to fulfill what was bound to me ages past."

"And what happens if we're 'unworthy'?" Tariq's voice was laced with sarcasm, but a flicker of genuine fear lingered behind his words.

The man's smile was faint, a shadow of amusement. "Then you will not leave."

A silence stretched between them, the weight of his words pressing down like the air before a storm. Amal took a steadying breath, her gaze unwavering. "Then we won't fail. We've come too far to turn back."

The man inclined his head, his expression almost approving. "We shall see, seeker. The path ahead is dark and full of trials. But you—" his gaze flicked between Amal and Tariq, "—you may yet surprise even me."

Without another word, he turned, slipping back into the shadows as if he'd never been there at all.

The air in the corridor felt different now, heavier, as if the walls themselves were listening. Tariq kept his gaze locked on the genie, his brow furrowed with suspicion. This stranger's presence seemed to thicken the shadows, and though he stood still, the man exuded a sense of barely restrained power, like an old flame waiting to reignite.

"What exactly are you doing here?" Tariq's voice was low but firm, edged with unease. "You say you're a 'keeper'—that you're here to 'observe'—but I don't buy it. If you're so bound to this place, then why show yourself to us now?"

The genie's dark eyes narrowed, a faint smile curling at the edge of his mouth. "A question born of suspicion. Good." His gaze settled on Tariq, as if he saw past his face, peering into something deeper. "But understand this, skeptic—my purpose is not for you to judge."

Tariq took a step closer, folding his arms. "So you're here to judge us, but we can't ask why? That doesn't sit right with me."

The genie tilted his head slightly, the shadow of amusement flickering in his eyes. "There is much about this world that does not sit right with mortals. I am but a part of this place, woven into its fabric. My purpose is bound to these ruins, and to those who wander through them."

"Enough with the riddles." Tariq's voice sharpened, his frustration bubbling over. "What do you gain from all this? Watching us stumble around, feeding us half-truths?"

"Gain?" The genie's smile faded, his gaze turning cold. "I am beyond such petty concerns. I am here because I was made to be here. To be an observer, a guardian. To watch and to wait."

"Wait for what?" Amal interrupted, her voice steady, her eyes fixed on him. "You keep talking about judgment and worth. Who decides? Is it you?"

"Not I alone," the genie replied, his gaze settling on her with a measure of respect. "But by the will of those who came before. Of those who left the Phoenix as a gift—and a curse."

"A curse?" Tariq's skepticism sharpened, his gaze flicking between the genie and Amal. "You hear that, Amal? Even he says it's a curse."

Amal's expression didn't waver. She stepped forward, meeting the genie's eyes without flinching. "Knowledge is only a curse for those who aren't prepared to wield it. We came here because we're ready—because we're worthy."

The genie chuckled softly, his voice a low rumble. "You believe worthiness is a matter of will? That determination alone grants you the right to possess what was sealed away?"

"It's more than just determination," she replied, her voice calm but fierce. "We understand the risks. We know what's at stake."

"Do you?" He leaned in slightly, his gaze piercing, as if searching for cracks in her resolve. "Do you understand that some knowledge is a burden too great? That there are truths which, once revealed, cannot be undone?"

Tariq watched, his jaw clenched, ready to step in, but he held back, sensing this was a test—not just of Amal, but of the bond between them. His gaze drifted to her, seeing the fire in her eyes, a fire that had burned brighter with every step deeper into these ruins.

Amal didn't flinch under the genie's gaze. "If there's knowledge here, then it's meant to be found. No one seals away secrets unless they're worth discovering."

The genie straightened, crossing his arms, his expression unreadable. "And what will you do if what you find isn't what you expect? If the Phoenix's power is as much a curse as it is a gift?"

"We'll face it," she replied firmly. "That's what we came here for."

A silence settled over them, thick and charged. Tariq felt his chest tighten, sensing a hidden weight in the genie's words. He wanted to argue, to pull Amal back, to make her see that this pursuit was more dangerous than even she realized. But he knew that look on her face—unyielding, unwavering.

The genie turned his gaze to Tariq, a hint of challenge in his expression. "And you, skeptic? Will you stand by her? Even if the path grows darker than you imagine?"

Tariq swallowed, glancing at Amal, then back at the genie. "I'm here because I gave my word. To my family, and to her. I don't walk away just because things get hard."

The genie's smile returned, softer this time, almost... approving. "Loyalty. A rare quality, even among seekers."

"I'm not a seeker," Tariq replied tersely. "I'm here because she's here. Because someone has to keep her grounded."

"Then perhaps you are wiser than you realize," the genie murmured, his gaze drifting back to Amal. "And perhaps... you will see that wisdom and strength are not always the same."

Amal crossed her arms, her gaze unwavering. "You don't think we're ready, do you? You think we're like all the others who came here and failed."

The genie shook his head slowly. "I do not think. I know what has happened before. And I know that there are many ways to be unworthy. Some fail by cowardice. Others by arrogance."

Tariq exhaled sharply. "Well, that's comforting."

"Fear not, skeptic," the genie replied with a small smirk. "I am neither your ally nor your enemy. I am simply... here. Bound by my role, to observe and to judge, but not to interfere."

"And if we need guidance?" Amal pressed.

He inclined his head, a faint smile returning. "Then perhaps you will find it... but not from me."

With that, he stepped back, his form melting into the shadows once more, leaving Amal and Tariq alone in the silence of the ancient hall. The echoes of his warnings lingered, an invisible weight pressing down on them, but Amal took a breath, steeling herself.

"We're going to prove him wrong," she murmured, her voice fierce.

Tariq didn't reply, but the resolve in his expression said enough.

The silence settled thickly after the genie's last words, stretching between them like a chasm. Amal and Tariq exchanged a wary glance, both aware that the man before them—if he even was a man—carried secrets older than they could fathom.

The genie's gaze lingered on the stones around them, his fingers tracing a faintly glowing line carved into the wall beside him. His touch was reverent, almost tender, as if each symbol held memories he alone could decipher. When he finally spoke, his voice was low, almost sorrowful.

"To seek the Phoenix," he murmured, eyes distant, "is to be judged. By the path, by the flame… and by those who came before."

Amal took a step closer, her expression intense, hungry for answers. "What do you mean, 'to be judged'? Judged by whom?"

The genie's gaze flicked to her, a faint smile curling at his lips, though it lacked warmth. "By the Phoenix itself… and by the ruin you stand in. You walk through a place that remembers."

"Remembers what?" Tariq asked, his tone cautious. He couldn't shake the feeling that this figure—this enigmatic, ageless presence—held more to him than mere words could convey. "What does this place remember?"

The genie's fingers stopped tracing, resting on a jagged, spiraling symbol near the center of the wall. "It remembers the seekers who came before. Those who craved power, those who sought understanding… and those who perished for daring to claim it."

"Perished?" Tariq echoed, unable to hide the note of alarm in his voice. "So you're saying we could—"

The genie's gaze held his, piercing and unyielding. "Yes. Many have tried. Few have succeeded. Fewer still left with anything but ashes in their hands."

"But you stayed," Amal pressed, her voice unshaken by his warning. "You've been here, bound by these ruins. Why?"

For the first time, the genie looked almost… pained. He turned his face away, his expression shadowed. "An ancient oath binds me to these stones, to these paths. My fate is tied to that of the Phoenix, as surely as the flame is tied to the air it consumes."

Amal's eyes narrowed, catching onto the solemnity of his words. "So you're trapped here. Forced to watch as others seek what you cannot take for yourself."

The genie's smile was bitter, an echo of something lost. "Perhaps. But I am here because I must be. And I am here to remind you—" he paused, his voice deepening, "—that paths like these are not to be walked without consequence. You, seekers, step onto ground that will judge every choice, every breath, every hesitation."

Tariq's eyes narrowed, sensing the genie's hidden struggle, an ancient weariness in his voice. "Then why stay? If this place only remembers sorrow and death, why not leave?"

The genie's gaze grew dark, a shadowed storm gathering in his eyes. "I do not stay by choice, skeptic. I am bound here by forces older than time. My fate is tied to the fate of those who pass through this place, to be their witness, their shadow, their… warning."

"Warning?" Tariq echoed, his tone edged with both disbelief and curiosity. "A warning of what?"

The genie turned to him, his face solemn, almost haunted. "That knowledge and power are as much a curse as they are a gift. That those who seek the Phoenix must be prepared to face what lies within themselves… and what they may lose in the process."

Amal took a breath, her eyes filled with determination. "We're prepared. Whatever test lies ahead, we'll face it."

The genie's gaze softened slightly, as if he saw something in her that resonated with an old, half-forgotten memory. "Brave words, seeker. But bravery alone is not enough. The Phoenix does not merely grant power. It reveals truth, and truth is often a harsher fate than death."

Tariq's voice was quieter now, laced with both caution and empathy. "You talk about it like you've seen it—like you've known the cost."

The genie's eyes darkened, his face unreadable. "Perhaps I have. And perhaps that is why I am here… to prevent others from making the same mistake."

"But we're different," Amal insisted, her voice unwavering. "We're not here out of greed. We're here to understand, to learn."

The genie let out a soft, humorless laugh, shaking his head. "Many before you said the same. You will forgive me if I do not take mortals at their word so easily. The Phoenix sees into the soul, into the deepest parts of a seeker's heart. It knows desire, fear, hope, and ambition. And it does not forgive weakness."

Silence fell, each word heavy with warning. Tariq shifted, his gaze intense. "So what is it you're saying? That we'll be tested?"

The genie nodded, his expression grim. "Not by me. Not even by the Phoenix alone. By the path itself. These walls are old; they remember failure. And they will test you, even as they tempt you with what you seek."

Amal set her jaw, her eyes alight with resolve. "We're ready."

The genie held her gaze, as if searching for something within her words. "We shall see, seeker. We shall see."

With that, he stepped back, his form fading into the shadows, his presence lingering in the cold air. The silence that followed was thicker, heavier, as if the walls themselves held their breath, waiting to see if these two seekers would prove worthy… or become just another memory.

Chapter 4
Shadows of the Past

The vast chamber opened up before them, barren and ghostly under the dim torchlight. In its center stood a single stone pillar, tall and weathered, its surface etched with symbols that seemed to ripple and shift in the faint stir of the desert wind that somehow reached them, even deep within this ancient city. The symbols danced across the pillar's face, moving with a rhythm that was unsettlingly alive, as though the stone itself breathed with the cadence of the winds outside.

Amal's eyes fixed on the pillar, her expression intense, calculating. She reached forward, her fingertips hovering just above the shifting symbols, not daring to touch but drawn irresistibly closer. Her brow furrowed, her mind racing through the fragments of ancient texts, forgotten legends, and hints of magic that she had spent her life piecing together.

"The answer lies in the wind," she murmured, almost in a trance. Her voice was soft but held a certainty that sent a shiver through Tariq, who stood just a few paces behind, watching her with a mixture of awe and apprehension.

"What does that mean?" Tariq asked, his voice breaking the thick silence. He studied the pillar, his instincts on edge. Every fiber of his being told him that this was no ordinary puzzle—that whatever lay hidden here demanded caution, not the reckless curiosity Amal exuded.

Amal glanced back at him, her eyes alight with that familiar fire of discovery. "It means we're dealing with ancient magic. This isn't just a riddle in stone; it's a riddle of the elements." She pointed at the symbols, watching as they seemed to drift and reform in patterns dictated by the faint desert breeze. "The wind shapes these symbols, shifts them, brings them to life. To solve this... we need to understand the wind's message."

The genie, standing in silent observation, narrowed his gaze at the pillar, his expression guarded. "This puzzle was crafted by those who understood the elements, who bound magic into stone and sand. The wind here does not merely blow; it whispers to those who can hear it."

Amal's lips pressed into a thin line of concentration. "And I can hear it," she murmured, stepping closer. Her eyes followed the shifting symbols with an intensity that bordered on reverence. "It's speaking to us... guiding us. We just need to listen."

Tariq frowned, his discomfort evident as he shifted his weight. "And what if we don't understand it? What if it's more than just a riddle? Something meant to keep us out, not invite us in?"

Amal gave him a small, reassuring smile, but it did little to ease his worry. "That's exactly why we have to figure it out. If they didn't want us to enter, they wouldn't have left a puzzle at all. This is a challenge, a test of our understanding."

He let out a sigh, his gaze flicking warily from her to the pillar. "Or it's a trap, one meant to catch those who think they can unlock the Phoenix's power."

Ignoring his concern, Amal turned her attention back to the pillar. She tilted her head, studying the symbols as they flowed in delicate patterns, weaving themselves into shapes that hinted at meaning but refused to hold still long enough to be fully understood. She closed her eyes briefly, breathing deeply, as though trying to attune herself to the invisible currents that shaped the symbols.

"It's like… each shift tells a story," she whispered. "A cycle, maybe. Beginning and end, life and death, like the Phoenix itself."

The genie's voice was quiet, almost reverent. "The Phoenix embodies rebirth through destruction. The wind may carry the same cycle—constant, changing, yet eternal. But be warned, Amal. Magic like this tests not only intellect but intent. It demands to know why you seek its secrets."

Amal glanced at him, a flicker of curiosity in her eyes. "And if we're worthy, the path will reveal itself. If not…"

"Then the sand will claim you as it has claimed all others," the genie replied simply.

Tariq felt his chest tighten, dread creeping up his spine as he regarded the pillar with renewed caution. "Amal, what if this is where we're supposed to stop? You heard him. If our intentions aren't enough, this could end here, in the dust."

But Amal's gaze remained steady, fixed on the pillar, her mind lost in the shifting patterns of symbols. "We didn't come all this way to stop here. We're closer than we've ever been, Tariq. The wind is trying to show us the way."

He looked at her, frustration mingling with a fierce loyalty that refused to let him abandon her, no matter how dark his instincts warned him this path would become. "All right. But let's be careful. We don't know what this magic demands from us."

She nodded, determination in her gaze. Amal reached out once more, her hand pausing just above the symbols, feeling the faint brush of wind as it circled around the pillar, as though inviting her to join in the dance. The symbols seemed to slow, aligning themselves into an almost comprehensible shape—a single, incomplete image hovering just out of reach.

In that moment, Amal felt a spark of understanding. She closed her eyes, letting the wind swirl around her, listening to its whispers, feeling the patterns of its movements. The answer was there, hidden within the rhythm of the air, a riddle woven from both stone and breeze, waiting to reveal itself to those who could perceive it.

And as she opened her eyes, she knew. The pillar's symbols shifted one last time, settling into place as she spoke the answer aloud, her voice firm, clear, and filled with conviction.

"It's not about control," she murmured. "It's about harmony."

A low rumble echoed through the chamber as the symbols on the pillar flared brightly, casting a warm light across the ancient stone walls. The wind grew stronger for a moment, swirling around them, then died down, leaving an expectant silence.

Amal stepped back, a triumphant gleam in her eyes as the stone pillar began to shift, revealing an opening just large enough to step through. She looked at Tariq, her face lit with both awe and resolve.

"The path forward," she said, her voice barely above a whisper. And though he didn't share her confidence, Tariq nodded, his trust in her overpowering his fears.

Together, they stepped through the opening, into the heart of the ancient city, deeper into the secrets of the Phoenix and whatever lay ahead.

The air had grown thick, almost oppressive, as Amal and Tariq moved through the narrow passageways, the walls around them seeming to close in with every step. The corridor twisted and turned like a labyrinth, its stone floors littered with fine sand that swirled in thin, restless eddies around their ankles. The faint sounds of distant winds reached them, a relentless whisper that seemed to be both guiding and mocking them at once.

Tariq's face was tight with concentration and rising anxiety. The sand beneath them was shifting more noticeably now, sloping unevenly, as if the ground itself was becoming unstable. He cast a wary glance at Amal, who remained focused, her brow furrowed as she traced her fingers along the latest set of intricate symbols etched into the walls.

"Amal," he said, his voice strained, "this feels wrong. The sand is moving under us. We can't keep pushing forward without knowing what we're risking."

She barely looked at him, her attention fixed on the carvings. "I know what I'm doing, Tariq. We're close. These symbols are part of the puzzle, and if we just understand the patterns, they'll guide us to the next step."

He exhaled sharply, trying to keep his temper in check. "But what if we're triggering something dangerous? What if this shifting sand is a warning?"

She finally turned to him, her gaze steady. "You saw what happened with the pillar. This place is testing us, Tariq, not trying to destroy us. It's a trial—a challenge to see if we're worthy of the Phoenix's secrets. If we stop now, we might lose our chance."

He shook his head, frustration mingling with fear. "Amal, that's exactly what worries me. The Phoenix's power isn't some ancient artifact we can just pick up and put on display. What if these 'tests' don't have an end? What if they're meant to trap us here forever?"

Amal smiled faintly, though there was a hint of impatience in her eyes. "That's not how these things work, Tariq. Every ancient civilization that revered the Phoenix left clues for those they deemed worthy. We've come this far because we're meant to. Trust me."

But her words did little to calm the growing sense of dread within him. The ground beneath their feet shifted again, and this time, it felt as though a great weight was settling into the stones, pressing down on them. The winds outside the walls howled louder, seeping into the passageways, their chilling whispers filling the air with an eerie sense of urgency.

"This doesn't feel like a test," he muttered, his gaze darting nervously to the floor, where the sand seemed to be gathering in spirals, like small whirlpools forming beneath them. "It feels like a countdown."

Amal hesitated, glancing down at the shifting sand. For a brief moment, doubt flickered in her eyes, but she quickly pushed it away, her resolve hardening. "We can't stop now, Tariq. There's no going back. We're too close."

He grabbed her arm, his voice low and tense. "Listen to me—this place isn't behaving normally. The walls are shifting, the sand is practically alive. What if solving this puzzle doesn't lead us to the Phoenix, but to something we can't handle?"

She shook his hand off gently, her expression softening. "Tariq, I know you're afraid. But we've faced risks before—countless times. Trust in me, just one more time."

The genie, who had been observing their exchange silently, finally spoke, his voice a low murmur that seemed to blend with the wind itself. "This place is old, ancient beyond your reckoning. It has a life of its own, a heartbeat of stone and sand. You may solve the puzzles, yes, but remember—this place has its own will. It chooses who leaves."

Amal glanced at him, her gaze unwavering. "And I intend to be one of those who do. The Phoenix's power is here, and I will not leave until we understand it."

Tariq's patience snapped, his voice rising. "Understand it? Amal, what if understanding it costs us everything? What if the Phoenix's 'power' is more than we're prepared to face?"

She looked back at him, her expression a mixture of determination and frustration. "Then you're free to turn back, Tariq. But I'm moving forward."

The ground shifted again, more forcefully this time, and a thin crack appeared beneath their feet, snaking its way through the sand-covered stone. The wind outside the chamber surged, and suddenly, the passage was filled with a soft rumble, the kind of sound that preludes a far greater disturbance.

Tariq's hand clenched, panic flickering in his eyes. "Amal, we need to decide—now. Either we press on, or we find a way out of here."

She looked at him, her gaze intense, yet filled with a kind of exhilaration that bordered on madness. "We press on. We have no choice now."

He wanted to argue, to pull her away, but he knew she would never turn back, not with the Phoenix's promise so close.

Instead, he swallowed his fear, his voice barely above a whisper. "Then let's make it fast."

Amal took a step forward, her eyes locked onto the next set of symbols that had emerged on the wall, their meaning faintly illuminated by the wavering torchlight. She reached out, her fingers hovering just over the carved surface, as if sensing the flow of magic that pulsed faintly beneath the stone.

"The symbols are forming words," she murmured, tracing the shapes with her fingertips. "They're pointing us to the final step."

Tariq's voice was tense. "Then hurry. I don't know how much longer this place will hold."

The sand beneath them churned, spilling over the crack in thin streams, almost as if the ground itself were bleeding. The genie's voice sounded again, calm but heavy with caution. "Remember, Amal—power is not granted without sacrifice."

She nodded, her eyes blazing as she whispered, "I know. But this is a risk I'm willing to take."

With that, she pressed her hand firmly against the stone, and the symbols flared to life, casting the passage in a blinding light. The rumble beneath them grew louder, the ground trembling violently as the winds howled through the corridor, their fury unleashed as if in protest.

For a moment, the world around them seemed to hold its breath, suspended in a fragile balance of stone, sand, and magic.

And then, with a sound like the breaking of the world itself, the stone beneath them began to shift, revealing a descending path shrouded in darkness, leading deeper into the ancient heart of the city.

Amal's expression was triumphant as she looked at Tariq, her face lit by the glow of the symbols. "This is it. The Phoenix awaits."

But as they stepped forward, Tariq could not shake the feeling that they had triggered something far more dangerous than they could ever have anticipated.

The chamber was quiet, the only sound the faint, eerie whistling of the wind as it slipped through unseen cracks and hidden crevices. Amal stood before the stone wall, her fingers hovering just above the shifting symbols, her gaze intense and unyielding. She felt the presence of something ancient, a magic that pulsed faintly in the air around her, guiding her in silent whispers.

The symbols before her shifted like grains of sand caught in a breeze, their movement erratic yet oddly purposeful. For a long time, she had tried to force them into meaning, searching for a logical connection, a pattern that would yield to reason. But it had taken a moment of stillness, a surrender to the nature of the riddle, for the answer to surface.

"It's the wind," she whispered, her voice filled with quiet revelation. "The answer is in the wind itself."

Tariq, who had been standing close by, watching with bated breath, glanced at her in confusion. "What do you mean?"

She turned to him, her eyes bright with sudden understanding. "The symbols—they aren't fixed. They're meant to move, to flow. I was trying to make them fit like pieces of a puzzle, but they're following the wind. They align only when you let them move with it."

He looked at her, a flicker of hope breaking through his tension. "So, if you let them align naturally..."

She nodded, reaching forward and gently brushing her hand against the stone. Instead of pressing down or forcing the symbols into place, she followed their movement, her fingers tracing the patterns as they shifted, letting them lead her. Each touch felt like connecting with an ancient memory, as if the wall itself was guiding her, recognizing her intent.

Slowly, the symbols began to settle, their chaotic movement merging into a single, cohesive pattern. A low rumble reverberated through the chamber, and the stone beneath their feet trembled slightly as the wall before them came to life, ancient gears grinding into motion. The symbols aligned at last, forming a single, intricate design that pulsed with a faint inner light.

With a deep, echoing groan, the wall began to shift. Stone slid against stone, revealing a dark passageway that stretched ahead, disappearing into shadows thick with mystery.

Tariq exhaled, relief washing over him as the tension in his body loosened. "Finally," he muttered, a faint smile crossing his face. "We're one step closer."

But the genie's expression remained tense, his gaze fixed on the darkened path before them, eyes filled with unspoken warning. "One puzzle solved," he said quietly, his voice carrying a somber edge, "but the real test has yet to come."

Amal's gaze flicked toward him, her confidence unwavering. "We've made it this far. Whatever lies ahead, we can handle it."

The genie's eyes darkened, his gaze cold and distant. "The path to the Phoenix is not laid out for the bold or the clever. It is laid out for those willing to sacrifice, those who can face their deepest fears without flinching. This puzzle was merely a gatekeeper—a small trial to determine your intent."

Tariq shifted uneasily, casting a wary glance at the passageway. "And what's waiting for us inside?"

The genie's voice was soft, barely above a whisper. "Truths that were never meant for mortal eyes. Power that is bound to life and death. What awaits you is not just discovery, but transformation. And it will cost more than you realize."

Amal's resolve held firm, her gaze steady. "I'm ready to face whatever it takes. I've dedicated my life to uncovering the truth, to understanding the power hidden in places like this. I won't be turned back by fear."

The genie's expression softened slightly, though a shadow of sadness lingered in his eyes. "Bravery is a noble thing, Amal. But it is not the same as wisdom."

He stepped back, gesturing toward the newly opened passage. "This is the path you have chosen. Beyond lies the heart of the Phoenix's domain, where the power you seek is waiting. But know this—the Phoenix does not share its secrets lightly. It demands something in return."

Tariq's gaze drifted from the genie to Amal, concern etched deeply into his face. "Are you sure about this? We don't know what kind of 'sacrifice' he's talking about. This could be more than just… another discovery."

Amal took a breath, her gaze steady and resolute. "I know what it could cost, Tariq. But I also know what we could gain. This isn't just about us. It's about understanding something that has been hidden from the world for centuries. I'm not going to walk away now."

For a long moment, the three of them stood in silence, the weight of Amal's words hanging in the air. The faint whistling of the wind seemed to echo her determination, a quiet song of persistence and purpose. Finally, Tariq nodded, though his expression was solemn, his eyes shadowed by worry.

"All right," he said softly, meeting her gaze with reluctant acceptance. "Then let's see this through."

They stepped forward together, their figures swallowed by the darkness of the passageway, the light of their torches flickering against the ancient stone walls. As they walked, the genie's words lingered in the air, a quiet, haunting reminder of the unknown trials that awaited them.

And as they ventured further into the heart of the Phoenix's realm, they felt the weight of an ancient presence, watching, waiting, a force as old as the desert winds themselves. The path had been unlocked, but the journey was far from over.

Chapter 5
The Trials Begin

The air in the chamber was still and cold, a silence that pressed in on Amal and Tariq like an unseen weight. Flickering light from their torches cast shadows over the ancient statues lining the walls, each figure frozen in a pose of contemplation, hands clasped around scrolls or open books. Symbols and inscriptions were carved into the stone, intricate patterns that twisted and turned across the chamber's walls, hinting at secrets buried for centuries.

"This... feels different," Tariq muttered, his voice echoing in the vast space. He glanced around warily, his eyes narrowing at the statues, as if expecting one of them to spring to life.

Amal stepped forward, her gaze tracing the carvings with intense focus. "Look at these symbols. They're not just decorative. They're instructions... or perhaps a warning."

Tariq huffed, adjusting his pack on his shoulder. "Instructions? So, we're supposed to read this ancient language and just know what to do?"

"Something like that," she replied, her tone distracted as she moved closer to one of the statues. Her fingers brushed over the surface of a stone tablet held in the statue's hands, feeling the etched lines beneath her fingertips. "These aren't just statues. They're... guardians, almost. Each one represents an aspect of knowledge, of wisdom."

"Wisdom?" He arched a skeptical brow. "So, what are we supposed to do—solve a riddle or recite ancient philosophy?"

Amal tilted her head, eyes narrowing as she studied the symbols on the tablet. "Maybe. Wisdom isn't just about knowing things. It's about understanding, about seeing beyond what's obvious. These trials… they're not going to be physical. They're going to test us in other ways."

Tariq crossed his arms, still skeptical. "Other ways? So, we're going to outsmart stone statues now?"

Amal shot him a brief, amused glance. "Something like that, yes. But these aren't just random statues. They're symbols of the Phoenix's nature—knowledge, restraint, balance. Each one holds a piece of what the Phoenix values in those who seek its power."

He looked at her, a touch of doubt in his eyes. "And you're sure about that?"

"As sure as I can be," she replied. "Look, the Phoenix isn't just a creature of fire. It's an embodiment of rebirth, of renewal. That doesn't come from brute strength. It comes from understanding, from wisdom."

"So… what?" He gestured around the room. "We're supposed to impress these stone guardians with our knowledge?"

Amal leaned in, examining a series of symbols on the wall beside the statue. She frowned, then nodded, as if coming to a decision. "It's a riddle. See these symbols? They're in patterns, not random. They ask a question—a question of purpose."

Tariq sighed, rubbing his temples. "I'm not following. A question of purpose?"

"Yes." She turned to face him fully, her voice steady and serious. "It's asking us why we're here, why we seek the Phoenix's power. If we answer without understanding, if we answer with arrogance or greed, we fail."

He scoffed softly. "You really believe that? That a... spirit or a magical bird cares why we're here?"

Amal's gaze was unwavering. "I believe that whatever force protects the Phoenix wants to know that its power will be respected. And if we don't show that, it will turn us away—or worse."

A beat of silence passed as Tariq considered her words, glancing back at the statues. Finally, he nodded, though reluctantly. "Alright. Let's say you're right. What kind of answer is it looking for?"

Amal turned back to the statue, her voice thoughtful. "It's looking for sincerity. For wisdom that goes beyond facts and knowledge, Tariq. We have to show that we understand what the Phoenix represents."

He sighed, feeling a strange mix of frustration and admiration. "So, what? We... answer its question? What do we say?"

She took a deep breath, closing her eyes as she gathered her thoughts. "Why do we seek the Phoenix? Because we believe in the power of renewal, in the possibility of transformation. Because we understand that true power is not just taken—it's earned."

Her words seemed to settle in the room, filling the silence. For a moment, nothing happened. But then, a faint glow appeared on the statue's tablet, illuminating the words as though they had been waiting for her answer.

Tariq watched in awe, the glow reflecting in his eyes. "It worked… you actually got it right."

Amal opened her eyes, her expression calm but satisfied. "Wisdom isn't just about being clever, Tariq. It's about seeing the heart of things. That's what this trial was testing."

He nodded slowly, his initial skepticism fading into something more respectful. "Alright, then. Lead the way, wise one. I'll follow your lead."

A smile touched her lips, but it was brief. She knew this was only the beginning.

The chamber shifted beneath their feet with a low rumble, sending a fine layer of dust cascading down from the ceiling. The walls, previously solid and immovable, seemed to ripple, shifting like the sands outside, revealing new patterns and symbols as they reformed into an intricate puzzle.

Tariq steadied himself, eyes wide. "What... what is happening?"

"It's part of the trial," Amal murmured, her gaze locked on the symbols reappearing across the chamber walls. "We're meant to see this through. It's testing us, Tariq."

"Testing us how?" His voice edged with a nervous energy as he watched her step closer to the symbols. "This feels more like a trap than a test."

"It's a test," she insisted, her eyes narrowing as she traced her fingers over a set of symbols carved into the wall. "Look here—these shapes, these patterns... they're not random. They're asking us to understand, to see beyond what's on the surface."

"Beyond the surface?" He shook his head, frowning. "Amal, they're just stones. How are we supposed to know what they mean?"

She glanced over her shoulder, a hint of excitement lighting up her eyes. "They're not just stones, Tariq. They're pieces of something larger. We need to align them, interpret what they represent."

"So, you're saying it's a puzzle?" Tariq's skepticism was clear, but he moved closer, reluctantly drawn in by her certainty.

"Yes," she replied, her tone urgent. "Look here." She pointed to a series of stones shaped like small crescents. "These represent phases, changes over time... transformations. And these—" she gestured to a set of jagged stones—"they're obstacles. We're meant to arrange them, to show an understanding of how challenges lead to growth."

He exhaled, glancing at her with doubt. "And if we get it wrong?"

Amal's voice was steady, but her eyes held a hint of caution. "Then we fail."

Tariq rubbed his forehead, staring at the stones as though they might offer some explanation. "Great. So we're here to interpret what exactly? The meaning of life?"

"Something close to it," she replied, a small, wry smile tugging at her lips. "The Phoenix isn't just about life or death. It's about renewal, change... resilience. If we show that we understand, that we respect the process, then we'll move forward."

He let out a slow breath, looking at her with a mixture of admiration and exasperation. "Alright. So where do we start?"

"Here," she said, pointing to a series of stones shaped like circles. "Circles represent cycles. Life, death, rebirth. We need to align them in a sequence that shows progression, something that signifies understanding."

"Understanding?" He echoed, his tone skeptical but softer now. "Alright, let's try it." He lifted one of the circular stones and moved it beside another, matching her movements as they aligned the pieces. "Like this?"

"Not quite," she said, adjusting the stones slightly. "Think about the phases—the beginning, the end, and what comes after. It's not linear. It's... cyclical."

"So... we're looking for balance?" he asked, starting to see a pattern in the seemingly random stones. "Each piece needs to reflect something in the next?"

"Yes!" Her face lit up, encouraging him. "Balance. Harmony. Each symbol reflects a part of the journey—one step leading to the next, each phase informing the other."

Tariq took a steadying breath, concentrating as he shifted another stone into place. "Like this, then?"

"Exactly," Amal replied, her tone softening with approval. "You're beginning to understand."

He glanced at her, a flicker of pride in his expression. "Don't sound so surprised."

She smiled, shifting another stone into position, and he could see the gleam of excitement in her eyes, the passion that had driven her all this way. "I knew you'd catch on."

Another rumble echoed through the chamber as they aligned the last stone, and the symbols along the walls began to glow faintly, casting a warm light around them.

Tariq took a step back, marveling at the sight. "So... this is it? We passed the test?"

Amal's gaze swept over the glowing symbols, her expression pensive. "Not entirely. It's more than just moving stones around. It's showing that we understand the journey they represent. We've only taken the first step."

Tariq sighed, his shoulders relaxing. "Well, at least that's something. But tell me, Amal… do you really believe all this? That the Phoenix, this path we're on, has a… purpose?"

She looked at him, her voice calm, but her eyes fierce with conviction. "Yes, I do. It's more than just legends or myths. This place, these symbols… they're part of something much bigger. The Phoenix represents understanding, but only for those who prove themselves worthy."

He held her gaze for a moment, absorbing her words. "Then let's prove it."

With a final, low rumble, the stones they had carefully aligned clicked into place. A soft glow emanated from the symbols on the wall, brightening gradually until the entire chamber was bathed in a warm, golden light. Tariq shielded his eyes, blinking against the sudden brightness as the walls seemed to shift, revealing an archway in the far corner of the room. Beyond it lay a shadowed passage, mysterious and inviting.

Amal's breath caught as she took a step closer, eyes fixed on the newly revealed path. "We did it… the first trial," she murmured, a note of awe in her voice.

Beside her, Tariq let out a slow breath, a mixture of relief and caution in his expression. "Alright, so we solved their riddle. Now what? Another trial?"

Before Amal could respond, a figure emerged from the shadows beside the archway, his presence commanding and oddly familiar. The genie's dark eyes glinted with quiet approval, a faint smile ghosting over his lips as he regarded them.

"You have passed the first test," he said, his voice smooth and resonant, carrying an air of ancient authority. "Wisdom. Understanding. Few make it this far."

Amal straightened, meeting the genie's gaze with confidence. "Then we've proven ourselves, haven't we? We're worthy of seeking the Phoenix."

The genie inclined his head slightly, an almost respectful gesture. "You have proven yourselves... thus far. But each step forward brings its own test, its own demand for something deeper."

Tariq's brow furrowed, his unease clear in the set of his jaw. "So what are these tests meant to do, exactly? Weed out those who aren't 'worthy'?"

The genie's gaze turned to him, unreadable and unwavering. "These trials are not meant to punish or harm. They are a reflection—of the Phoenix's nature, of the journey that those who seek it must undertake. They sift the shallow from the determined, the greedy from the wise."

Amal's eyes gleamed with renewed determination. "Then each trial is a step closer. A step toward proving ourselves worthy of understanding the Phoenix."

"Yes," the genie replied, nodding. "The Phoenix does not reveal itself to those who come seeking power alone. It is wisdom, resilience, self-knowledge. Only those who grasp these concepts may approach it."

Tariq crossed his arms, glancing back at the chamber with a doubtful frown. "So if we're not worthy, these trials… what, reject us? Kill us?"

The genie's expression softened, though a hint of warning lingered in his gaze. "They will reveal your weaknesses, expose the shadows within you. Some are able to face them; others…" He paused, allowing his silence to fill in the gravity of his words. "Others turn back. Or are turned back."

Tariq's frown deepened, but he nodded, accepting the genie's words with wary respect. "Alright, so we keep going. What's the next trial?"

The genie didn't answer immediately, his eyes returning to Amal. "You are eager, seeker," he observed, a trace of something almost like admiration in his tone. "But remember, eagerness can lead to folly. Do not rush ahead without understanding the purpose of each step."

Amal met his gaze squarely, a spark of defiance in her eyes. "I know why I'm here. Each trial, each step… it's all part of proving that. We came here to find the Phoenix, to understand its power and purpose, and that's exactly what we'll do."

The genie's smile grew faintly, almost imperceptibly. "We shall see, seeker." He looked between them, his expression shifting to something close to a blessing, though shadowed by a deep-seated caution. "For now, the path is open. Proceed with wisdom and care. The trials will guide you… and judge you."

With that, he took a step back, fading once more into the shadows, leaving the archway open and waiting. Tariq glanced at the space where the genie had stood, a wary expression lingering in his eyes.

"He just… vanished," Tariq murmured, half to himself. "Like he's part of this place, as much as the walls or the stones."

Amal placed a hand on his shoulder, her voice steady. "He's a guardian of these ruins, Tariq. He's bound to them, but he's also guiding us. In a way, he's part of the Phoenix's test too."

Tariq exhaled, his unease still visible. "And you trust him? After everything he's warned us about?"

"It's not about trust," she replied softly, her gaze drifting to the archway, the faint glow within seeming to beckon them forward. "It's about understanding. The trials, the warnings… they're all part of what the Phoenix represents. And if we're here, then we're meant to face it all."

A flicker of something passed over Tariq's face—apprehension mixed with reluctant acceptance. "Fine. But don't forget that these trials aren't just puzzles. They're meant to test us, to push us to our limits."

Amal nodded, a faint smile on her lips. "Then let's meet those limits head-on."

With a shared look of resolve, they turned to the archway. The path ahead was shrouded in shadows, but as they stepped forward, the chamber's glow seemed to follow them, illuminating the first few steps of their journey into the unknown. The air felt charged with an energy that was both daunting and exhilarating, as if the walls themselves were holding their breath, waiting to see if these two seekers would prove worthy—or be consumed by the trials that lay ahead.

Chapter 6
Echoes of the Forgotten

They had found a small clearing within the ruins, open to the vast night sky. The stars overhead were like distant embers scattered across a dark, velvet canopy, illuminating the ancient stone around them with a silvery glow. The air was still, heavy with the scent of the desert at night, and for a rare moment, the ruins were silent. Amal and Tariq sat close to the remains of a low wall, their tired bodies relaxing against the cool stone, their gazes drawn skyward.

The genie stood apart, silent, his eyes distant as he stared into the stars. His expression was unreadable, yet there was a heaviness in his stance, an unmistakable tension that seemed to deepen with each passing day. Tariq noticed, and with a glance at Amal, he cleared his throat, his voice breaking the silence.

"You've been awfully quiet tonight," Tariq said, his tone light but his gaze intent. "Not that you're the chatty type, but something's different. You're... distracted."

The genie's gaze didn't shift from the stars, though his expression grew taut. "Even the quietest desert holds whispers," he murmured. "Some whispers carry more weight than others."

Amal leaned forward, her curiosity sparking. "You've been here before, haven't you?" she asked, her voice softer. "I mean... you seem to know this place in a way that goes beyond just guiding us. There's a familiarity in your eyes."

The genie hesitated, his face tightening as though he were wrestling with an old, buried memory. Finally, he let out a sigh, his shoulders sagging slightly. "I suppose it is time," he said quietly, more to himself than to them. He turned to face them, the starlight casting a ghostly glow over his features, making his eyes seem deeper, filled with ages of history and secrets.

"What do you mean?" Tariq asked, a hint of wariness creeping into his voice.

The genie looked at them both, his expression somber. "This place, this city, was once my home. I was part of the civilization that built these halls, carved these walls, and forged the very fire you now wield. We revered the Phoenix, dedicated our lives to understanding its power, its cycle of creation and destruction."

Amal's eyes widened, her expression a mix of shock and fascination. "You… you were one of them? The people who built this city?" Her voice dropped to a reverent whisper. "I had no idea."

He nodded slowly, his gaze distant as though looking back through centuries. "Yes. I was once as human as you are now. But time… time can strip a soul of many things. Memories fade, emotions dull, until all that remains is purpose." He paused, his eyes darkening. "And my purpose was bound by magic to protect the secrets of this city, to ensure they would not fall into the wrong hands."

Tariq exchanged a wary glance with Amal, his skepticism obvious. "So, you're saying you were… trapped here? Forced to guard this place for centuries? By choice?"

A bitter smile flickered across the genie's face. "Choice," he repeated, his tone hollow. "My choice was to protect what we had created. We believed we were safeguarding something precious, something too powerful for the unprepared. And yet, I had not foreseen the cost."

Amal leaned closer, her voice soft with empathy. "But why? Why would you bind yourself like this, for so long, knowing you'd be… alone?"

He met her gaze, his eyes hardening. "Because I believed in the Phoenix's power. We all did. We saw it as a force that could reshape the world, a source of life and death bound together in perfect harmony. But as our knowledge grew, so did our fears. There were those who wanted the Phoenix's power for themselves, to wield it without understanding its price. And so, to protect it, we chose guardianship over freedom."

Tariq frowned, his tone wary. "And now that we're here, unlocking these puzzles, touching the Phoenix's magic… how does that sit with you?"

The genie's face remained impassive, though there was a flicker of something in his gaze—something close to sorrow. "It troubles me, Tariq. Your journey awakens memories I thought long buried. I am bound to this place, to its purpose, yet you…

you represent something I never anticipated. A chance for the Phoenix to rise once more."

Amal's voice was gentle, almost hesitant. "And do you believe we're ready? That we deserve to know its secrets?"

The genie's eyes softened, his voice barely a whisper. "The Phoenix does not judge by merit alone. It seeks those willing to sacrifice, to embrace both the light and the shadow of its power. But as for readiness…" He paused, his gaze piercing. "That is something only the fire can decide."

Tariq's voice was low, laced with doubt. "And if we're not ready? What happens then?"

The genie looked at him, his face unreadable. "Then you will face the Phoenix's wrath. For power without understanding is a curse, not a gift."

Amal sat quietly, the weight of his words settling over her like a heavy cloak. Her fingers instinctively brushed over the brazier they had lit hours before, feeling the faint warmth still pulsing within it. "You were one of them," she murmured, almost to herself. "And yet, you're here now, guiding us. Do you regret it?"

The genie's face softened, a sadness filling his gaze. "There was a time when I did. When the weight of centuries felt like a punishment, a prison from which there was no escape. But you…" He looked at Amal, his voice thick with an emotion he rarely showed. "You remind me of what we once sought, of the passion that drove us. Perhaps that is why I am here, why I guide you now. Because in you, I see the hope of something more—an understanding that eluded us."

Tariq's voice was almost a whisper. "And if we do succeed? If we unlock the Phoenix's power… what then?"

The genie's gaze was steady, his voice filled with a quiet, resolute strength. "Then you will face a choice. To wield it wisely, or to let it consume you. But remember this: the Phoenix is both fire and ash. Creation and destruction are inseparable, and the path you choose will define the fate of all who come after."

They sat in silence, the weight of his revelation pressing down on them. Above, the stars continued their slow, timeless journey across the sky, indifferent to the lives below. For the first time, the siblings felt the full scope of what lay ahead—not just a discovery, but a reckoning. And as they looked at the genie, the centuries of duty and sacrifice etched into his face, they understood that their guide was more than just a guardian. He was a reminder of the price they might one day pay.

The fire crackled softly, its light casting shifting shadows on the ancient stone walls around them. Tariq's face was tense, his expression a storm of anger and betrayal. He clenched his fists, his voice a low growl as he looked at the genie.

"So, you knew all along," he spat, his voice barely controlled. "You knew what we were getting into, and you didn't tell us. You guided us through these puzzles, let us get closer to this…

this dangerous power, and never once did you think to warn us?"

The genie's face was impassive, his eyes downcast, shadowed with regret. "Would you have listened if I had? Or would you have dismissed my words as easily as you do now?"

Tariq took a step closer, his gaze blazing with fury. "Don't try to twist this. You lied to us! You led us into something that could end us—and for what? Some ancient duty you can't seem to let go of?"

Amal's voice was softer, conflicted, yet filled with tension. "But why hide it from us?" she asked, her eyes fixed on the genie, her voice a mixture of hurt and confusion. "You told us stories, warned us about the Phoenix's power, but never… never the truth. That you were one of them, part of this city. That you're bound to the Phoenix."

The genie's eyes met hers, his expression solemn. "Because the truth is more dangerous than you know, Amal. I kept it from you because I wanted you to approach the Phoenix without preconceived fears, without the shadow of my past hanging over your choices. The Phoenix's power is meant to test, to reveal what lies within. Knowing too much… can corrupt that path."

Tariq scoffed, his voice laced with disdain. "How convenient for you. You get to cling to your 'duty,' while we walk blindly into something that could kill us."

The genie's gaze darkened, a flicker of old pain surfacing in his eyes. "You think this is easy for me? You think watching you both awaken the same dangerous power that destroyed my people is something I do lightly?" His voice dropped, filled with a quiet sorrow. "I have watched over this place for centuries, knowing that the day would come when someone, perhaps even someone worthy, would attempt to claim the Phoenix's secrets. And I have feared that day as much as I have hoped for it."

Amal took a step forward, her voice trembling with emotion. "So, you're saying… that we're not just unlocking knowledge? That we're risking more than our lives?"

The genie's expression softened as he looked at her, a sadness filling his gaze. "Yes. The Phoenix's power is not simply a force to wield; it is a force that transforms, that demands a sacrifice. To awaken it fully is to challenge the balance that holds our world together. It could end everything you know, everything you are. And it could end… even me."

Tariq's jaw clenched, the weight of the revelation pressing down on him. "So, if we go forward, we're risking… what, exactly? The whole city? The desert? All of us?"

"Not just yourselves, but the world beyond these sands," the genie replied, his voice a grave whisper. "The Phoenix's fire is more than magic. It is life and death bound together, an eternal cycle. To disrupt it is to risk plunging the world into chaos."

Amal's face paled, the enormity of his words sinking in. "Then... why are you helping us? Why not stop us outright?"

"Because I am bound to guide those who enter this place," the genie said quietly. "I am bound to the Phoenix, its power, and its purpose. But the choice... the choice to awaken it lies with you."

Tariq let out a harsh breath, his frustration boiling over. "This is madness. We're standing here, on the brink of something we don't fully understand, and all we have to go on is your word. Your word, from someone who's led us into more danger than we bargained for."

The genie's gaze did not falter. "Believe me or not, it changes nothing. The Phoenix's power will test you both, whether you realize it or not. I have tried to prepare you, to protect you in the ways I could, but I cannot stop you. You came here seeking answers. Now you must be prepared to face them."

Amal looked away, her voice soft with regret. "But this changes everything. I thought... I thought we were here to discover, to learn something that could help others. I didn't come here to bring destruction."

The genie's face softened, his expression filled with a sad understanding. "Sometimes, Amal, discovery and destruction are two sides of the same coin. Knowledge is not always a gift. Sometimes, it is a burden."

Tariq crossed his arms, his gaze unwavering. "Then tell us what happens if we stop. If we turn back now, leave everything as it is. What happens then?"

The genie's voice grew softer, almost wistful. "Then the Phoenix will remain undisturbed, its power bound to this place, as it has been for centuries. And I will continue to guard these ruins, waiting… until another arrives, drawn by the same curiosity, the same desire for truth. The cycle will begin again."

Amal's eyes filled with conflicted emotion as she looked at the genie. "And that's what you want? To be left here, forever tied to this place, waiting for others to come?"

He sighed, the weight of centuries clear in his voice. "It is not what I want, Amal. But it is what I chose long ago. I chose to guard this place, knowing that one day, someone might succeed where we failed. And yet, each time, I wonder… if they truly understand the cost."

Tariq's voice softened, a flicker of sympathy breaking through his anger. "Then tell us. Tell us what we're truly risking. No more half-truths, no more stories. Just… the truth."

The genie looked at them both, his expression filled with an unspoken sorrow. "You are risking your lives, yes. But more than that, you are risking the delicate balance that keeps this world from unraveling. If you awaken the Phoenix's power, you may lose yourselves to it. And if you are not careful… it may take from you everything you hold dear."

They sat in silence, the enormity of his words settling over them like a heavy shroud. Above them, the stars continued their slow, indifferent journey across the sky, bearing witness to the choice that lay before them.

The silence after the genie's revelation was as heavy as the desert night itself. Amal stared at the faintly glowing fire in the brazier, her mind racing with the weight of their decision. Tariq sat across from her, his arms crossed tightly, his gaze shifting restlessly from the genie to the distant shadows beyond the firelight.

Finally, Tariq broke the silence, his voice rough with frustration. "You still want to go forward, don't you?"

Amal looked up, her eyes steady. "Yes, I do." She spoke with conviction, yet there was a tremor in her voice, a sign that she, too, felt the magnitude of what lay ahead. "We came here for answers, Tariq. The Phoenix's power—whatever it is—might be the key to something greater than we understand."

Tariq scoffed, his tone sharp. "Greater than we understand? Amal, that's exactly the problem. We *don't* understand. And you just heard him"—he gestured toward the genie—"the risks aren't just about us. They could affect everyone. This place wasn't meant to be disturbed."

She shook her head, her frustration mirroring his. "But isn't that what discovery is? Facing the unknown, even if it's dangerous? This knowledge... it was hidden for a reason, yes, but maybe that reason was fear. Fear of change, fear of power—"

"Or fear of destruction!" Tariq interrupted, his voice louder than he intended. He took a breath, visibly calming himself, but his eyes remained fierce. "You're talking about change as if it's something controllable, something we can harness. But the Phoenix isn't just a relic or a tool, Amal. It's a force, and if we can't control it, we're putting everything at risk."

The genie watched them quietly, his face solemn. "Your brother speaks with caution, Amal. He is not wrong to question what you seek. Many before you desired the Phoenix's power and lost everything in the attempt."

Amal's jaw tightened, her eyes flashing with determination. "I respect the risk. But I also know that fear has kept people from the truth for too long. We didn't travel across the desert, solve these puzzles, and come this far just to walk away now. This isn't just about power, Tariq. It's about understanding."

Tariq threw up his hands, his voice tinged with exasperation. "And at what cost, Amal? What's the point of knowledge if it destroys us to gain it? This isn't just some academic pursuit, it's—"

"It's my life's work!" Her voice cut through his, sharp and unyielding. "You know that, Tariq. You've always known that." She paused, her voice softening. "I don't want to lose you in this, but I can't walk away."

He looked away, his face a mix of pain and anger. "And I can't lose you. I can't stand by and watch you risk your life—both of our lives—for something we can't even be sure we'll survive." He met her gaze, his tone pleading. "I'm asking you, Amal. Let's leave this. We can still turn back."

She stared at him, her face softening, but her resolve held firm. "I'm sorry, Tariq. But I have to see this through."

The genie shifted, his presence a reminder of the history they now found themselves entangled in. "Perhaps," he began slowly, "the two of you are both right, in different ways. The Phoenix's magic does not yield lightly. It demands both courage and caution. And neither of you can succeed without the other."

Amal's gaze flickered toward him, her brow furrowing. "Then what are you saying? That we must both face this, but differently?"

The genie nodded, his tone quiet but firm. "Yes. Amal, your passion for discovery is the key that unlocks doors. But, Tariq, your caution may be the anchor that keeps you both from losing yourselves. You came as allies. Do not let the Phoenix's trials tear you apart."

Tariq's eyes narrowed, his voice filled with skepticism. "You think one speech can make us forget everything you've hidden from us? You kept us in the dark about the risks, about your past. And now you want us to trust your guidance?"

The genie looked at him, a flicker of sorrow passing through his gaze. "My duty is to protect this place, to ensure its secrets are not misused. But my duty does not require me to make your decisions for you. You must choose your path."

Amal's voice softened, her eyes pleading as she looked at Tariq. "Tariq, I need you by my side. I can't do this alone. And I don't want to. Please. I know the risks, but we have each other, and I believe that will be enough."

He looked at her, his face conflicted, torn between loyalty to his sister and his own deep-seated fear. "Amal, I… I don't want to lose you to this."

"You won't," she whispered, her voice steady. "We'll face it together."

The genie's gaze moved between them, his voice a murmur filled with ancient wisdom. "Together, you will be stronger. But if you walk this path divided, the Phoenix will sense it. And it will devour whatever weakness it finds."

Tariq sighed, finally nodding, though reluctance still lingered in his eyes. "Fine. But I swear, Amal, the second I see that this is going too far, we stop. Agreed?"

She managed a faint smile, her expression both grateful and determined. "Agreed."

As they settled back into silence, the gravity of the path before them weighed heavily on each of them. Their fates were bound now, not only to each other but to the ancient magic they sought to uncover. And with every step forward, the genie's words echoed in their minds—a reminder that the Phoenix's power was as much a force of creation as it was of destruction, and it would spare neither if they failed to face it together.

Chapter 7
Symbols and Secrets

The chamber stretched before them in a long, shadowed expanse, the walls covered from floor to ceiling with dense, interwoven symbols. Intricate patterns danced along the stone, spiraling and branching out into complex shapes, each line telling a story as old as the stones themselves. The dim torchlight cast shadows over the markings, bringing them to life in flickering waves as if the symbols pulsed with hidden knowledge.

Amal moved with measured purpose, her eyes scanning the symbols as she walked. Her fingers hovered near the carvings, tracing the air just above the stones. There was something in her expression—an intense, almost reverent focus—that held Tariq's attention. He stayed a step behind, observing her with newfound respect as she began murmuring to herself, piecing together the patterns with a sense of familiarity.

"These symbols... they're fragments of a language I studied years ago," she said, her voice soft but confident. "I never thought I'd see it in an actual structure."

Tariq raised an eyebrow, genuinely intrigued. "You recognize this? I thought these symbols were lost to time or... just another legend."

Amal smiled faintly, her gaze never leaving the wall. "Most of them are. This language is ancient, predating nearly every known civilization. I studied pieces of it in old manuscripts, fragments of lore that survived through oral tradition. But seeing it here, carved into stone—this is beyond what I could have imagined."

She paused at a section of the wall where the symbols formed an elaborate spiral, each loop leading seamlessly into the next. Her fingers grazed the carvings, following the intricate lines with a delicate touch. "This," she murmured, "this is part of the Phoenix's lore. These symbols... they represent stages of transformation—birth, death, rebirth. It's all here."

Tariq watched her, a mix of surprise and curiosity on his face. "So, all those years of you buried in texts and scrolls... this is what you were working toward?"

Amal glanced over at him, a glint of pride in her eyes. "Yes, though I never knew if I'd get the chance to actually see it. I've spent years learning fragments of this language, piecing together myths, studying ancient dialects that barely survived the ages. Most of my knowledge came from incomplete records, texts that had been damaged or lost. But now..." She gestured at the wall, her expression a mixture of awe and satisfaction. "Now, it's all here, preserved as it was meant to be."

As she continued moving along the wall, Amal pointed to a specific series of symbols that curved inward, forming a series of concentric circles. "Look at these," she said, her voice tinged with excitement. "These symbols here—they're phonetic markers, like a key to translating the surrounding text. In the manuscripts, I'd only ever seen isolated versions of these. They function as a guide, anchoring the reader to the core message of the text."

Tariq's gaze followed her hand, trying to see what she saw. To him, the symbols seemed like indecipherable lines, almost too intricate to be anything more than abstract designs. But seeing her expression, the intensity in her eyes as she interpreted the symbols, he felt a glimmer of understanding—a sense that these markings held meaning beyond their appearance, that they were a language waiting for her to unlock.

"So what do they mean?" he asked, a trace of respect in his voice.

Amal's eyes softened, her tone shifting to a quiet, reverent cadence. "They speak of cycles. Renewal. The nature of change. The Phoenix embodies these qualities, and these symbols… they serve as a reminder of that. They aren't just words; they're a philosophy, a way of seeing the world. To understand them is to understand the heart of the Phoenix itself."

She moved to another section, where the symbols grew sharper, more angular. Her fingers hesitated over the jagged lines, her brow furrowing as she read their meaning. "These are warnings," she murmured, her voice barely above a whisper. "Warnings to those who seek the Phoenix's power for themselves, rather than for understanding. The language becomes harsh, almost violent. It's a reminder… a barrier."

Tariq watched her, struck by the ease with which she deciphered these symbols that seemed so foreign to him. "How do you do it?" he asked quietly. "You make it seem… natural."

Amal smiled faintly, a touch of humility softening her gaze. "It's not natural—it's years of study. Hours of pouring over texts, memorizing fragments, cross-referencing symbols from different cultures and eras. I trained myself to see patterns, to feel out meanings even when the words were lost. I didn't realize how much I'd learned until… well, until now."

He nodded slowly, his skepticism fading as he watched her work. "Guess I didn't fully appreciate what all those late nights were for."

She chuckled softly, her fingers still tracing the wall. "You always thought I was just obsessed. But this… this is more than an obsession, Tariq. It's a calling. To piece together fragments, to understand the voices of those who came before us. It's like stepping into their world, seeing it through their eyes."

Tariq looked around, suddenly aware of the gravity of the moment. This wasn't just an ancient ruin to Amal—it was a testament to her life's work, to the dedication that had brought her here. "Well," he said, his voice softened, "if anyone can bring these voices to life, it's you."

Amal's expression warmed, and she met his gaze, gratitude flickering in her eyes. "Thank you," she said quietly. "That means more than you know."

Turning back to the wall, she inhaled deeply, her focus sharpening as she absorbed the symbols, her mind piecing together meanings, connections, and histories. The markings no longer felt like isolated symbols; they were a language, a story, revealing themselves to her one phrase at a time.

In that moment, Tariq felt a renewed sense of faith—not in the symbols or the myths, but in her. For the first time, he realized the strength it had taken to reach this place, the resolve she'd honed through years of study and solitude. Whatever trials lay ahead, he felt certain that, with Amal's knowledge and determination, they were ready to face them together.

The symbols stretched across the wall in an unbroken line, winding around pillars and disappearing into shadowed alcoves. Each section seemed to shift subtly, patterns transforming as the light played over the stone, revealing connections that weren't visible at first glance. Amal's gaze swept over them, her brows knit with concentration, but her steps slowed as the symbols grew more complex, more layered.

She pressed her lips together, tracing her finger along a particularly convoluted design that spiraled inward before branching off in opposing directions. "This… this part doesn't make sense," she muttered, mostly to herself, her tone laced with frustration. "It should follow the previous sequence, but it's… different. Deliberately broken."

Tariq peered over her shoulder, squinting at the wall. "So, what's that mean? Someone messed up the engraving?"

Amal shook her head, half-smiling at his suggestion. "No, it's intentional. This culture valued precision. Breaking a sequence like this would have been done to make a point... but what point?" She trailed off, her fingers hovering over the symbols as if hoping they'd reveal their secrets with a touch.

Silence fell between them as she studied the patterns, and Tariq noticed a flicker of hesitation in her eyes—a rare sight in someone usually so assured in her work. He leaned against the wall, watching her, sensing her uncertainty.

"You're not... stuck, are you?" he asked, his voice gentle but teasing.

She glanced at him, a rueful smile crossing her face. "I might be," she admitted, her shoulders sinking just slightly. "It's not that I can't understand it. It's just... some things don't translate. Not fully. There are meanings here that don't fit into words or even the symbols we know."

Tariq raised an eyebrow. "But isn't that why you came? Because you wanted to uncover meanings others missed?"

"Yes, but—" She paused, exhaling slowly. "I'm not always certain, Tariq. Sometimes I'm just... guessing. Piecing fragments together and hoping they make sense. And there's always this nagging feeling that I'm missing something, that I'll never quite see it all."

He studied her, a flicker of admiration in his gaze. "You make it look easy, though. Like you were born understanding all this. I didn't think you ever... doubted yourself."

A quiet laugh escaped her. "I'm constantly doubting myself. Every time I think I'm close, it's like the answers slip away, leaving just enough behind to keep me going. But that's part of the thrill, isn't it? The idea that there's always more to discover, more to learn."

Tariq's eyes softened, his tone reflective. "That's what keeps you moving forward, even when the rest of us would've given up."

"Maybe," she murmured, turning back to the wall, her fingers brushing the symbols as though reacquainting herself with them. "It's... humbling, actually. The more I learn, the more I realize how much I don't know. Every time I decode a symbol, I find five more that contradict it or add layers I hadn't even considered."

She fell silent, studying a line of symbols shaped like interlocking spirals, her gaze drifting as she tried to make sense of the patterns. Tariq waited, watching her, and couldn't help but feel a swell of respect. For Amal, this wasn't just a puzzle to solve—it was a commitment, a passion rooted in something far deeper than simple curiosity.

After a long pause, she finally spoke, her voice low. "Look at these spirals here. They're familiar, but... something about them is different. They're almost distorted, like they're hiding part of their meaning."

"Or maybe the meaning's supposed to be hidden," Tariq suggested, watching her intently. "Like you said, they wouldn't break a pattern unless they wanted to make a point."

She glanced at him, nodding slowly. "You're right. It's almost like they're trying to force the viewer to see it from a different perspective. Maybe…" She took a step back, angling her head to view the symbols from a distance. "Maybe they're not meant to be read up close. Sometimes a pattern only reveals itself from a distance."

Tariq stepped back with her, tilting his head. "Alright, professor. Show me the bigger picture."

She chuckled, a bit of color returning to her cheeks. "Watch and learn." She focused, following the spirals until they connected to a broader section of the wall, where the patterns curved together, creating the shape of a flame—a hidden depiction of the Phoenix, rising from the symbols themselves.

"There it is," she whispered, almost to herself. "The Phoenix… it's embedded in the language itself, like a signature."

Tariq's eyes widened, impressed. "You did it, Amal. You actually saw it. And here I thought you were just making guesses."

Her laughter was soft, self-deprecating. "Half of this is guesses, Tariq. Educated ones, maybe, but guesses all the same. But…

every so often, it clicks." She looked at him, her eyes shining with a mixture of relief and excitement. "And that's what makes it worth it. That moment when the pieces fit together, and I finally see the whole picture."

He nodded, an understanding smile spreading across his face. "Well, then, keep guessing. Seems like you're good at it."

Her gaze softened, and for a moment, they stood there in quiet appreciation of the discovery, the hidden Phoenix watching over them from its place on the wall. Amal reached up to touch it lightly, as if the symbol itself were a kindred spirit, one she'd been searching for all her life.

"Let's keep moving," she said, her voice quiet but determined. "There's more to uncover. And maybe, just maybe, we'll get it right."

Tariq nodded, ready to follow. As they stepped away from the hidden Phoenix and deeper into the chamber, he couldn't help but feel that this journey was transforming her—giving her the chance to not only find the answers she sought, but to become the person she'd always aspired to be.

Amal knelt before a row of symbols carved in delicate, swirling patterns across the stone, her fingers hovering above them as if they were sacred. She traced the intricate curves, her eyes alight with something beyond mere fascination—this was reverence, discovery, the fulfillment of years of searching finally coming into focus.

"These symbols," she murmured, her voice trembling slightly, "they're different from the others. They're… a story." She leaned closer, her gaze intense as she followed the lines, her voice growing in strength and certainty. "This is part of the Phoenix's myth. I can feel it."

Tariq shifted behind her, watching with growing unease. "Amal, we're venturing pretty deep here. Are you sure we should be… unearthing this?"

Amal glanced back, her eyes gleaming with a fierce determination. "That's why we're here, Tariq. To understand what others have overlooked or abandoned. This myth—it's the key to everything we've been studying, everything I've worked toward."

He held her gaze, his brow furrowed. "And what if there's a reason it was abandoned? Hidden? Not every secret is meant to be found."

She turned back to the wall, brushing his caution aside, her voice calm but resolute. "Knowledge is never meant to be hidden. The truth needs to be uncovered, even if it's uncomfortable. This—" she gestured at the wall, her eyes fixed on the symbols, "—this was left here for someone to find."

Tariq sighed, rubbing the back of his neck. "Maybe. Or maybe it was left as a warning. Remember what the genie said—these symbols, these trials, they're meant to test us. To see if we're… worthy."

"And that's exactly what we're doing," Amal replied, turning back to him with a small smile, her expression softening just a bit. "We're proving ourselves. Don't you see, Tariq? The Phoenix isn't just a legend. It's a symbol of rebirth, of knowledge transcending time."

He exhaled slowly, his doubt lingering but his admiration evident. "You really believe that, don't you?"

She nodded, her expression intense. "I do. This myth, these symbols—they're part of something larger, something that connects us to the past and guides us forward. If I can understand this… if I can bring this knowledge to life, then everything I've sacrificed will have been worth it."

Tariq's eyes softened, and he took a step closer, his tone quieter. "Amal… just promise me you'll be careful. This isn't just academic curiosity anymore. We're dealing with something… powerful. Something that's been kept from the world for a reason."

She met his gaze, her own softening in response. "I know, Tariq. And I'm not doing this lightly. But if we stop now, if we walk away, then we'll never know. We'll never understand the truth behind these legends."

He hesitated, glancing back at the shadowed chamber behind them, the silence pressing in like a weight. "Alright. I'll follow your lead. But if things start feeling… wrong, we stop. Agreed?"

"Agreed," she said, her voice barely above a whisper. But even as she said it, her focus returned to the symbols, her gaze locked onto a sequence of spirals that looped together, forming the outline of a bird rising from flames.

"This," she breathed, pointing to the symbol, "is the Phoenix itself. It's telling us… about rebirth. About transformation." Her fingers traced the spirals, her expression shifting as she decoded the meaning embedded within the shapes. "It's not just about the physical. This myth—it's about the soul, about enduring through loss, through destruction, and emerging… changed."

Tariq's expression turned wary, his voice laced with concern. "And what if that change isn't something we can handle?"

She looked back at him, her gaze steady. "Then we face it together. The Phoenix's story is about resilience, Tariq. About understanding that every challenge, every trial, reshapes us. That's why this myth matters. It's not just a legend—it's a lesson."

A silence stretched between them, charged with an unspoken understanding. Tariq took a deep breath, nodding slowly as he saw the conviction in her eyes. "Alright. I'm with you. Just… let's stay alert."

She nodded, her expression softening. "Thank you." She turned back to the wall, her fingers resting on the carved outline of the Phoenix. For a moment, she closed her eyes, letting the weight of the symbols settle over her like a tangible presence.

Here, in the depths of this ancient ruin, she felt a kinship with the myth itself, a quiet understanding that transcended words.

The Phoenix—its trials, its teachings, its story—felt like a guide, a path she was meant to follow. She opened her eyes, her resolve hardening, her purpose clearer than ever.

"Let's go," she said, her voice steady, and together, they stepped deeper into the chamber, prepared to face whatever lay ahead.

Chapter 8
Bound by Oath

The sun was a fierce, blinding eye in the sky as Amal, Tariq, and the genie crested the ridge of the Scorched Mountains. The air was thick with sulfur, and the landscape stretched out before them in a seemingly endless expanse of jagged rock and smoldering cracks that exhaled thin wisps of steam. The land itself looked as though it had been burnt to ash and reborn a thousand times over, and the heat radiating from the ground made each step feel like a trial.

Amal shielded her eyes, taking in the harsh terrain with a determined expression. "This is it," she said, her voice firm. "The Scorched Mountains. Where the Phoenix's flame first ignited."

Tariq stopped, his face flushed from the exertion and the heat. He squinted into the distance, frowning. "And what exactly are we supposed to find here? These mountains are more dangerous than anything we've faced. If there was ever a place meant to keep secrets buried, it's this."

The genie, standing silent and watchful beside them, nodded in agreement. "These mountains hold power, yes. But they also hold death. The Phoenix's flame was not kind to this land, and its remnants linger in the very stones."

Amal turned to him, her eyes blazing with purpose. "You've been here before, haven't you? You know what we need to find."

The genie's gaze remained steady. "I was here long ago, before the Phoenix's power scorched the land. Before these peaks became a monument to flame and fury. But now… even I cannot say what remains."

Tariq shook his head, his expression filled with doubt. "So we're just supposed to wander through this wasteland, hoping we stumble across something that's been hidden for centuries? Amal, we've already lost so much. Are you sure this is worth it?"

She looked at him, her expression softening as she saw the exhaustion and worry etched on his face. "Tariq, I know you're tired. I am too. But we're close. I can feel it. Every step we take is a step closer to understanding the Phoenix, to honoring everything we've sacrificed. This isn't the time to turn back."

He let out a long sigh, glancing away toward the horizon. "It's not that I want to turn back. I just don't know if I trust what we're walking toward. I mean, look at this place." He gestured to the volcanic landscape, where fissures snaked through the earth, and the air shimmered with waves of heat. "It doesn't look like it's hiding answers, Amal. It looks like it's hiding a grave."

The genie's voice was calm, though there was an edge to it. "And yet, every legend, every relic leads here. The Scorched Mountains are where it all began. The Phoenix rose here, and it was here that it left its mark upon the world."

Amal glanced back at the genie, a flicker of understanding passing between them. "You still believe in it, don't you? Even after all this time, even after everything you've seen."

The genie inclined his head, his gaze unreadable. "Belief is a strange thing, Amal. It fades, but it does not vanish. I know the risks, perhaps better than either of you. But the Phoenix's fire is a truth I have lived with for centuries. And if it can be understood… then it must be."

Tariq crossed his arms, his skepticism clear. "Must it? Or is that just what you've told yourself after so many years trapped in that city? This could be nothing more than a curse we're digging up."

Amal shook her head, her voice fierce with conviction. "A curse is hidden out of fear. But the Phoenix was hidden out of reverence, Tariq. It's not just a legend; it's a part of this world, of everything around us. And I'm not leaving until we find the truth."

Tariq's shoulders slumped slightly, the fight draining out of him. "Fine. We keep going. But the second it feels like we're stepping into something we can't handle, I'm dragging you out of here. I don't care what secrets are left behind."

She managed a faint smile. "I wouldn't expect anything less."

They began their descent, the rocky ground crunching beneath their feet as they made their way through the heart of the Scorched Mountains. Every so often, a rumble would vibrate through the rocks, a reminder of the restless power simmering below.

Tariq broke the silence, his voice softer. "Amal... when did this all become so important to you? It's like... sometimes I look at you, and I don't even recognize the person you've become."

She looked back at him, her expression conflicted but resolute. "It's always been important to me, Tariq. Maybe I didn't know it back then, but... this is my purpose. Discovering the Phoenix, understanding what it left behind—it's like every step we take brings me closer to something I've been searching for my whole life."

He nodded, though there was a shadow of sadness in his gaze. "I just hope you find what you're looking for. And that it's worth what we've lost."

The genie's voice, low and grave, drifted through the oppressive heat. "The Phoenix's fire is both a blessing and a curse, Tariq. It reveals truths, but it demands a price. The question is not whether it's worth it, but whether you're prepared to pay that price."

Amal met the genie's gaze, her expression unwavering. "We've come this far. Whatever the price, I'll pay it."

Tariq's voice was almost a whisper. "And what if that price is everything, Amal? What if it takes more than we have to give?"

She looked forward, her voice steady but filled with a quiet determination. "Then we'll give everything. Because some truths are worth the cost, no matter what lies at the end of this path."

The three of them moved forward into the harsh landscape, their shadows stretching long over the scorched earth, each step echoing with the promise of discovery—and the threat of destruction.

They entered a cavern deep within the Scorched Mountains, where the air was thick with heat and the walls glowed with faint, ember-like veins that pulsed in time with some hidden, ancient heartbeat. At the center of the chamber rested a pedestal carved from volcanic stone, atop which sat a strange, twisted artifact. It was a metallic object, dark and scarred with scorch marks, yet it shimmered faintly with an inner fire. Amal approached it slowly, her gaze riveted by the glinting metal that seemed almost alive.

Tariq held her back, his hand firm on her shoulder. "Amal, wait. We don't know what that is. It could be another trap."

She looked back at him, her eyes alight with an intensity that bordered on obsession. "It's not a trap, Tariq. It's… calling to me." She turned back to the artifact, feeling a strange warmth fill her chest as she reached out. "I can feel it. This is tied to the Phoenix's flame."

The genie's voice came from behind them, quiet but laden with caution. "Be careful, Amal. Artifacts bound to the Phoenix's magic do not yield easily. They are alive with flame, and that flame consumes as much as it gives."

Amal hesitated, but only for a moment. Her fingers brushed against the metal, and as she touched it, a surge of warmth radiated up her arm, filling her with a strange, exhilarating energy. The artifact's veins glowed brighter, responding to her touch, and she could feel the magic pulsing beneath her skin.

Tariq's voice wavered, caught between awe and fear. "What… what's happening?"

She looked at him, her voice steady but filled with wonder. "It's responding to me. I don't know how, but I can feel the Phoenix's power—its fire. It's like it's waiting for something."

"Or someone," the genie murmured, his eyes shadowed. "Only those who are bound to the Phoenix can harness its artifacts without suffering the cost. But Amal… be wary. These artifacts demand loyalty. Once you accept this power, there is no turning back."

Amal met his gaze, her expression resolute. "I'm ready. If this is what we need to unlock the Phoenix's secrets, then I'll do it."

Tariq's hand tightened on her shoulder. "Amal, please. We've already lost Jibril. Do you really want to risk losing yourself too?"

Her face softened, but her determination remained unbroken. "I don't want to lose anything, Tariq. But this is our path. We're not meant to turn back." She turned back to the artifact, watching as the symbols etched into it began to shift, aligning in a complex pattern that hinted at the language of flame.

The genie stepped closer, his voice low. "The puzzle will reveal itself through the magic. But Amal, heed this warning: the Phoenix's flame is as much destruction as it is life. To awaken it fully could mean devastation beyond what you imagine."

She paused, her fingers hovering over the artifact. "Then... why would this be here? Why would the Phoenix's followers create something so dangerous?"

The genie's eyes darkened. "Because they believed in its balance. They believed that those who sought the Phoenix's power would understand that balance—or be destroyed by it. If you are to continue, you must accept that same balance."

Tariq's voice was pleading. "Amal, you don't have to do this. Let's leave this thing alone and get out of here while we still can."

She looked at him, her voice quiet but filled with a fierce resolve. "And if we do, if we walk away now, then we'll never know what we've left behind. All of this—Jibril's sacrifice, everything we've faced—it will have meant nothing." She turned her gaze back to the artifact, her fingers tracing its symbols as they shifted beneath her touch. "I won't turn back now."

The artifact pulsed, a bright surge of flame illuminating the chamber as its magic responded to her words, swirling into intricate patterns that twisted and turned in the air. She closed her eyes, feeling the energy flow through her, each symbol unraveling like pieces of a long-forgotten puzzle.

Tariq took a step back, watching her with a mixture of fear and admiration. "Amal… what are you doing?"

She opened her eyes, the flames reflected in her gaze. "I'm unlocking it. This is a part of the Phoenix, a part of its essence. It's telling me… showing me something." Her voice trailed off, mesmerized, as the flames danced around her, forming shapes and symbols that hinted at ancient secrets.

The genie watched her, his expression solemn. "You've bonded with it, Amal. But remember—the power of the Phoenix comes with a cost. If you awaken it, you must be prepared to pay that price."

She nodded slowly, her gaze unwavering. "I understand. I'm willing to face whatever comes."

Tariq's voice was barely a whisper. "And what if that price is everything?"

She looked at him, the flicker of flame casting shadows over her face. "Then we give everything. This is our destiny, Tariq. We didn't come here to walk away empty-handed."

The artifact flared one last time, then dimmed, leaving a faint, warm glow in its place as Amal stepped back, the symbols fading but leaving a lingering warmth in her hand. The air around them settled, the energy dissipating as the artifact returned to its dormant state.

The genie's voice was a soft warning, his gaze filled with unspoken knowledge. "You have taken the first step, but be wary. The path of fire is as treacherous as it is powerful. And the Phoenix's flame does not spare those who waver."

Amal looked back at him, her voice steady but tinged with awe. "I won't waver. Whatever comes next... I'm ready."

Tariq's face was pale, his eyes filled with a mixture of fear and loyalty. "Then so am I. But, Amal... remember what's at stake. If we lose each other to this, there's no one left to pull us back."

Amal took his hand, her grip firm. "We'll face it together, Tariq. Whatever the cost." And as they moved deeper into the heart of the Scorched Mountains, the weight of her words hung between them, a promise bound by the flame they had chosen to awaken.

The air crackled as Amal's hand hovered over the artifact, flames coiling around her fingertips like serpents eager to strike. The artifact's power had awakened, filling the cavern with a fierce, throbbing heat that radiated from Amal's very skin. But before she could marvel at the depth of the magic flowing through her, a familiar, chilling voice echoed from the shadows.

"So, you truly mean to wield it," Iskar said, his voice laced with contempt. "A foolish choice, Amal."

Amal spun around, her hand still alight with fire, her gaze defiant. "Iskar. I should've known you wouldn't stay away."

Iskar stepped forward, the members of the Ashen Veil closing in around them, their dark cloaks blending with the shadows. "Did you think we would let you walk out of here with the Phoenix's flame? This power was meant to remain buried—away from the reckless hands of mortals."

Tariq stepped closer to Amal, his voice taut with barely restrained anger. "We're not here to destroy anything. We're here to understand. Unlike you, we believe this power has a purpose beyond secrecy and control."

Iskar's gaze turned to him, cold and unyielding. "Then you're a fool, Tariq. Power such as this corrupts. Look at her." He gestured to Amal, whose skin glistened with the heat of the magic she had absorbed. "Already, the fire consumes her. Soon, she'll be little more than an ember, burning for the sake of a power she can't control."

Amal's eyes narrowed, flames dancing in her palm. "I am in control. You just don't understand the Phoenix's power because you're too afraid of what it could mean."

"Afraid?" Iskar scoffed, his voice filled with disdain. "I fear only what this power will unleash if left unchecked. You're blinded by curiosity, Amal. This path leads only to ruin, for you and everyone you hold dear."

Tariq's hand tightened on his sword, his voice low and fierce. "Maybe we'd believe you if you hadn't hunted us from the start. You've been trying to stop us, to keep the Phoenix's secrets locked away—no matter the cost."

Iskar's expression hardened, his voice a quiet, deadly murmur. "Then let this be the final warning, Tariq. Step aside, or be consumed along with her."

Amal raised her hand, the flames flaring higher. "If you want to stop us, Iskar, you'll have to go through me."

Iskar's lips twisted into a grim smile. "As you wish."

With a swift signal, the members of the Ashen Veil surged forward, their cloaks swirling like shadows in the firelight. Amal's eyes blazed as she extended her hand, the flames leaping from her fingertips and forming a wall of fire between them and the Veil's forces.

"Amal, wait!" Tariq shouted, alarm flashing in his eyes as he saw the strain on her face. "This magic—it's draining you!"

She gritted her teeth, her voice strained but determined. "I can handle it, Tariq. We have to get out of here!"

Iskar's voice called through the flames, mocking and relentless. "You're only prolonging the inevitable, Amal. You cannot control the Phoenix's fire forever. It will devour you."

Amal glared, her voice cutting through the roar of the flames. "I'll worry about that later. Right now, I just need enough to get us out."

Tariq's hand rested on her shoulder, his grip firm, his voice filled with worry. "At what cost, Amal? Look at you—you're pushing yourself too hard. You're becoming... I don't even know. This isn't you."

She hesitated, the flames flickering as her gaze met his. "Tariq, please. Trust me. We're so close, and if we don't keep moving, they'll stop us here. I can do this."

Iskar's cold laughter echoed from beyond the fire. "Hear him, Amal. Your brother understands better than you do. That fire in your hands is as much a curse as it is a power. The more you rely on it, the more it consumes you."

Tariq's voice grew desperate. "Amal, he's right. I've seen what this is doing to you, the way it's... changing you."

Her jaw clenched, defiance shining in her eyes as she held his gaze. "I'm still me, Tariq. This fire—it's part of me now. I'm not going to let it control me. I'll use it to protect us."

Iskar's voice cut through the roar of the flames like a knife. "Then you have already chosen your fate. Your stubbornness will be your undoing."

With a fierce yell, Amal thrust her hand forward, the flames blazing higher, forcing the Ashen Veil to retreat. The cavern shook with the intensity of the fire as it crackled and surged, a living barrier between them and their pursuers.

Tariq took her arm, his voice filled with urgency. "Amal, that's enough! We have to go, now!"

She nodded, though the exhaustion in her eyes was clear. "Right. Let's move."

Together, they turned and fled deeper into the cavern, the flames receding as Amal lowered her hand, though wisps of fire still clung to her fingertips. Behind them, the Ashen Veil regrouped, their voices fading as the distance between them grew.

As they reached a quiet pocket of the mountain, Tariq stopped, turning to face her, his expression tight with worry. "Amal, look at yourself. You're pale, exhausted. You're letting that fire drain you."

She took a shaky breath, her voice soft but resolute. "It's what we have to do, Tariq. I won't let them stop us. I can control it. I know I can."

He shook his head, his gaze filled with a mix of fear and frustration. "But for how long? How much of yourself are you willing to lose before you realize this isn't the way?"

She hesitated, but then lifted her chin, her voice steadier. "As much as it takes. Jibril gave his life for this, Tariq. We can't let them stop us now."

Tariq's voice softened, a shadow of sorrow in his eyes. "And what if it costs you more than you're willing to give?"

Amal looked at him, her gaze unyielding but laced with an undercurrent of uncertainty. "Then… I'll face that cost when it comes."

They stood in silence, the faint glow of firelight fading from her fingers, leaving a quiet darkness between them that was filled with more than just shadows.

Chapter 9
Unseen Forces

Iskar and his apprentice crouched within the shadow of a crumbling archway, their figures hidden by the deepening gloom. From their vantage point, they could see Amal and Tariq moving slowly along the ancient corridor, torchlight casting flickering shadows against the walls. Iskar's gaze was intense yet calm, his expression unreadable as he watched the two seekers navigate the chamber.

The apprentice shifted restlessly beside him, his young face etched with frustration. "Master, they are getting too close. If they reach the inner sanctum, there's no telling what they might awaken. Should we not act?"

Iskar's gaze remained fixed on Amal and Tariq, his voice steady. "We are not here to interfere, only to observe."

The apprentice let out an exasperated sigh, his voice low but insistent. "Observe? While they stumble toward secrets that could destroy them—and everything else? How can you be so calm?"

"Calm?" Iskar finally turned, his dark eyes narrowing slightly. "It is not calm, but resolve. We are bound by an oath, by rules that were set long before you or I. The Phoenix's secrets are not ours to guard through interference, only through vigilance."

The apprentice clenched his fists, his gaze flicking back to the figures of Amal and Tariq in the distance. "But they don't know the risks. They think this is some… treasure hunt, some quest for knowledge. They have no idea what the Phoenix's power could do."

"And it is not our duty to enlighten them," Iskar replied, his tone laced with a quiet finality. "Our duty is to protect the knowledge and allow only those who prove themselves to reach it."

The apprentice shook his head, his voice tinged with disbelief. "And what if they prove themselves, Master? What if they awaken something even they cannot control?"

Iskar's gaze softened, his voice dropping to a murmur. "Then it is their burden to bear, not ours. Every seeker is drawn by the promise of knowledge, of power, but few understand the price. Those who fail are turned away; those who succeed must be willing to pay that price."

"But what if that price is too high?" The apprentice's voice cracked with a mixture of fear and defiance. "What if the Phoenix's power doesn't stop with them? What if it spreads, unchecked?"

Iskar's expression grew darker, his voice firm but laced with an almost fatherly patience. "Then they will face the consequences. We cannot shape their path, only observe it. The moment we interfere, we undermine the very balance we are here to uphold."

The apprentice fell silent, absorbing his master's words. His gaze lingered on Amal and Tariq, his expression a blend of frustration and reluctant acceptance. "I don't understand why we must stand back and watch when we could prevent disaster."

"Because interference taints purpose," Iskar replied, his gaze steady. "The Phoenix is not a prize to be won lightly. Those who seek it must be tested—not just in courage, but in wisdom, restraint, and purpose. If we protect them from the dangers, we rob them of that test, and the Phoenix loses its true guardians."

The apprentice frowned, his voice softening, though uncertainty remained in his eyes. "And if they fail? If they are unworthy?"

"Then they will find only ash," Iskar said quietly, his voice holding a solemn weight. "And we will remain, as we always have, watching from the shadows. Protecting not by action, but by presence."

For a moment, they watched Amal and Tariq in silence, the flickering torchlight casting brief glimpses of their determined faces. The apprentice's gaze softened as he watched Amal, a hint of admiration creeping into his expression. "They are… different, aren't they? I've seen many seekers, but these two… they don't seem driven by greed or arrogance."

Iskar nodded slowly, his voice thoughtful. "Perhaps. But difference alone does not make one worthy. It is their understanding of what they seek that matters, their willingness to accept the consequences of their search."

The apprentice hesitated, glancing back at his master. "And if they are worthy? What then?"

Iskar's gaze grew distant, as if looking beyond the present moment, beyond the walls of the ancient ruins. "Then they will claim the Phoenix's power... or be consumed by it. But that decision is not ours to make. We are bound to watch, to witness their choices without interference. That is the purpose of the Ashen Veil."

The apprentice sighed, his voice laced with resignation. "I hope they understand the stakes, Master. I hope they're ready for what lies ahead."

Iskar's eyes flickered with a rare hint of empathy. "We can only hope, my student. Each seeker walks their path alone. And we... we are the keepers of that path, the watchers of the flame."

They fell silent again, each lost in their own thoughts as they continued to observe from the shadows.

The low murmur of footsteps echoed through the stone corridors, distant but drawing closer. Amal and Tariq's silhouettes shifted in and out of sight as they advanced, the faint glow of their torchlight casting shadows that danced along the walls.

The apprentice paced back and forth, glancing anxiously down the hallway where the seekers had disappeared. His hands clenched into fists, and his voice was edged with frustration as he turned to Iskar. "Master, they're getting too close. Every step they take… it's as if they're being led directly to the heart of this place."

Iskar watched him with a calm, unwavering gaze. "Patience," he said softly. "Our role has never been to obstruct, only to observe. They have not reached the threshold."

The apprentice shook his head, his voice raising slightly. "How can you be so indifferent? They don't understand what they're dealing with! If they reach the Phoenix, if they awaken it without true understanding…" He trailed off, swallowing as if the mere thought left a bitter taste in his mouth. "It could undo everything."

"We are bound, my apprentice. Bound by oath to remain in the shadows unless necessity compels us otherwise," Iskar replied, his voice carrying the weight of centuries. "They have yet to cross that line."

The apprentice exhaled sharply, looking away. "I know the oath, Master. I understand it as well as you do, but can't you see? They're walking into something they can't handle, something that could destroy them and the balance we're sworn to protect."

Iskar's gaze remained steady, almost pitying. "You let fear cloud your judgment. Fear for them… or fear of the Phoenix itself?"

The apprentice's eyes narrowed. "It's not fear—it's caution. Caution for what might happen if they take that power without respect or understanding. How many seekers have come before them, Master? How many have fallen?"

"Many," Iskar acknowledged, his tone even. "And each one failed for the same reasons—arrogance, haste, greed. But this pair… they are different."

"Different?" the apprentice scoffed, his tone laced with doubt. "They are still mortal, still fallible. Different doesn't make them worthy."

"No," Iskar agreed. "It does not. But that judgment is not ours to make. We are bound to watch, to allow their path to unfold without interference."

The apprentice's frustration boiled over, his voice rising. "Then what are we, if not protectors? What good is our oath if we sit by and do nothing while the Phoenix's power could be unleashed on a world unprepared for it?"

Iskar regarded him, his expression unchanging. "We are guardians of knowledge, not its gatekeepers. Our purpose is to bear witness, not to control. To interfere would be to corrupt the very purpose we have sworn to uphold."

The apprentice clenched his fists tighter, his voice laced with desperation. "So we do nothing? We watch them stumble toward disaster, and we call it 'honoring the oath'? Is that what it means to be part of the Ashen Veil?"

Iskar's gaze softened, a trace of empathy flickering in his eyes. "To be part of the Veil is to understand that knowledge is not ours to hoard. We are entrusted to guard it, yes, but also to let it be claimed by those who prove themselves. Knowledge untested is knowledge wasted."

"But what if they fail?" The apprentice's voice was quieter now, almost a plea. "What if they reach the Phoenix, and they can't handle what they find?"

"Then it will be as it always has been," Iskar said with quiet finality. "The Phoenix chooses its own guardians. Those who are unworthy will turn back or be consumed by their own limitations."

The apprentice let out a bitter laugh. "And if they don't turn back? If they aren't consumed?"

Iskar's eyes met his, unflinching. "Then they will inherit the Phoenix's power, and with it, the responsibility it demands. And we, as the Veil, will continue to watch, to remember, to preserve the balance as we always have."

The apprentice shook his head, his face tight with resentment. "I don't know how you do it, Master. How you stay so… detached. They're closer than anyone's been in years. How can you just… let them go on?"

Iskar placed a hand on the apprentice's shoulder, his voice a low murmur. "Detachment is not the absence of care. It is understanding the role we play. There is no true wisdom without letting go of control. The Phoenix's power is not ours to keep, nor to deny."

The apprentice's shoulders sagged, his voice little more than a whisper. "I just... I don't want to see them destroyed."

Iskar's expression softened, a brief flash of sympathy in his eyes. "Nor do I. But we cannot protect them from what they must face alone. Remember, the Phoenix is not just a creature of fire—it is a creature of rebirth, of transformation. If they are meant to endure, they will. And if they are not..." He paused, letting the weight of his words sink in.

The apprentice swallowed, nodding reluctantly. "Then we watch."

"Yes," Iskar replied, his tone resolute. "Then we watch, as we always have. That is the burden and the honor of the Veil."

The apprentice glanced back down the corridor, where the distant glow of Amal and Tariq's torches had almost disappeared around a corner. "I hope they understand what they're stepping into."

Iskar's gaze followed his, thoughtful and unwavering. "If they do not, the Phoenix will teach them. And that is a lesson no interference of ours can alter."

With a final, reluctant nod, the apprentice accepted his master's words, his frustration cooling to a simmering acceptance.

The dim passage stretched ahead, its silence thick and oppressive. Amal and Tariq moved cautiously, their footsteps echoing softly off the stone walls. Tariq glanced around, a hint of unease in his eyes, while Amal pressed forward, her gaze fixed and determined.

Then, from the shadows, a figure materialized, cloaked in a dark robe that seemed to blend into the very walls around him. Iskar's presence was as quiet as a whisper but as solid as the stone itself. His sudden appearance brought both Amal and Tariq to a halt, Tariq's hand instinctively reaching for Amal's arm.

"Who—" Tariq began, but Iskar raised a single hand, silencing him.

"You walk a path that was hidden for a reason," Iskar intoned, his voice low and resonant. His gaze settled on Amal, who stood her ground, undeterred.

Amal tilted her head, curiosity sparking in her eyes. "We know the risks. We wouldn't be here if we didn't understand what we're seeking."

Iskar's lips curled slightly, a shadow of a smile that held no warmth. "You may think you understand, but knowledge from afar and the weight of experience are not the same. This place... it remembers every seeker, every intention, every failure."

"Then let us add something new to its memory," Amal replied, her tone steady. "We're prepared for whatever trials lie ahead."

Iskar's gaze flickered over her, unreadable. "Prepared? I wonder if you truly know what that means." His voice grew softer, almost a murmur. "The Phoenix is no simple legend. It is both a gift and a trial. Those who seek it must be willing to confront what lies within themselves... and what they are willing to lose."

Tariq's grip on Amal's arm tightened. "What exactly are you warning us about?"

Iskar's gaze shifted to Tariq, his expression grave. "This journey you undertake will test you in ways that go beyond the physical. It will dig into your mind, your spirit, your very essence. There is no preparing for it—only facing it as it unfolds."

Amal crossed her arms, unfazed. "If that's meant to scare us, it's not working. We came here knowing we'd face dangers."

"Dangers?" Iskar repeated, a dark glint in his eye. "You think of this as a mere perilous journey? Then you are unprepared. The Phoenix does not test courage alone. It probes deeper, finds weaknesses, fears, secrets. It does not forgive weakness, nor does it tolerate ignorance."

Tariq took a step forward, his voice a mix of anxiety and determination. "So what are you saying? That we'll be judged? That… that it's already decided if we're worthy or not?"

Iskar inclined his head slightly. "No judgment is final until it is earned. The Phoenix sees all, feels all. It measures not just your actions, but your reasons, your convictions. Those who falter do not simply turn back. They lose something of themselves in the attempt."

Amal rolled her eyes, crossing her arms. "We've faced risks before. This is no different."

A faint trace of disappointment shadowed Iskar's face. "Risks? Foolishness. You speak of this as if it is a challenge that can be won through stubbornness alone." He stepped closer, his eyes narrowing. "Do not confuse bravery with wisdom, seeker. The Phoenix demands both."

Tariq swallowed, glancing uneasily at Amal. "Maybe we should listen, Amal. I mean… if he's right, if there's something we're missing…"

Amal waved him off, her gaze unwavering. "We've come too far to be frightened off by cryptic warnings. We know what we're after, and we know why."

Iskar's gaze lingered on her, and for a moment, a flicker of sadness passed through his expression. "Many have spoken those same words before you. And yet, the ruins hold only the echoes of their promises."

Tariq's face paled slightly. "What… what happened to them?"

"Some turned back, realizing the weight of the burden was beyond them," Iskar replied, his voice low. "Others pressed on, and in their arrogance… they were consumed by the very thing they sought."

"Consumed?" Tariq echoed, his voice barely above a whisper.

"Yes," Iskar said, his gaze piercing. "Their ambitions overtook their wisdom, their desire outpaced their caution. The Phoenix demands balance. Those who disrupt that balance find themselves… lost."

Amal lifted her chin defiantly. "Then we'll keep our balance. We'll prove ourselves, not to you, but to the Phoenix."

Iskar looked at her with a mixture of respect and regret. "It is not proving that matters, but understanding. The Phoenix is not simply won; it is accepted by those who seek truth, not glory."

Amal's voice was unwavering. "Then we're exactly where we need to be."

Iskar turned his gaze from her to Tariq, his voice softening slightly. "Remember this moment, skeptic. When the path darkens and doubt finds you, remember that turning back is a choice. The Phoenix will test everything within you; not all who begin this journey reach its end whole."

Tariq's grip tightened, his voice low. "We'll be careful."

Iskar nodded, the flicker of a knowing look passing over his face. "For your sake, I hope that caution holds. But know this—caution alone will not be enough. There will be choices, sacrifices, and those choices will not wait for you to be ready."

Amal met his gaze one last time, her tone firm. "We're ready. Whatever trials come, we're not turning back."

Iskar inclined his head slightly, a subtle acknowledgment. "Then may your courage match your conviction. For there will be a moment when courage is all you have left."

With that, he stepped back, fading into the shadows as silently as he had come, his figure disappearing into the dimness, leaving only his words echoing in the heavy silence. Amal stood firm, but Tariq felt the weight of the warning settle deep within him, a quiet, persistent unease.

For the first time, he wondered if they were truly ready for what awaited them.

Chapter 10
The Flame's Price

The grand temple loomed before them, its massive stone columns reaching up toward the cavernous ceiling as though seeking to touch the heavens. The air was thick with a tangible sense of anticipation, humming with ancient energy that pulsed in time with their footsteps. At the center of the chamber lay a sprawling mosaic, each tile an intricate piece of a larger, mysterious design that seemed to shift and change beneath the torchlight.

Amal stepped forward, her eyes wide as she took in the beauty and complexity of the mosaic. The tiles depicted the cycle of the Phoenix, each image more detailed than the last: a golden bird rising from flames, ash settling into new life, fire transforming into something transcendent. She could feel the weight of each tile's history, its meaning deeply embedded in the very fabric of the city.

"This..." she murmured, her voice barely above a whisper, "this is it. The final puzzle."

Tariq moved to stand beside her, his gaze wary as he took in the intricate patterns. "So, what are we supposed to do with it? Just stare until the answers appear?"

Amal knelt down, her fingers lightly brushing the cool stone. "No, it's more than that. This mosaic... it's a map, a story. Each tile connects to the next, like steps in a ritual." She glanced up at Nour and the genie, her eyes shining with a mixture of excitement and dread. "If we follow the sequence correctly, it should unlock… something."

Nour's face was serious, her gaze fixed on the mosaic as though she too could feel the pulse of power beneath it. "The Phoenix's cycle. Each stage must be acknowledged, respected, before it can be unlocked. It is a path of sacrifice and rebirth."

Tariq's expression darkened, his eyes darting to Amal. "Sacrifice. That's what worries me. Amal, if this puzzle is anything like the others… what exactly are we risking to solve it?"

She looked at him, her face softened by an understanding of his fear but resolute all the same. "We're risking what we always were, Tariq. To unlock the Phoenix's power means we step into its cycle—to understand it, to be part of it. We knew from the start it would be dangerous."

He exhaled, rubbing the back of his neck. "And how are we supposed to know when enough is enough? That this power, whatever it is, won't just take and take until we're gone?"

The genie stepped forward, his voice calm and measured. "There is no true understanding without cost, Tariq. The Phoenix was never about half-measures. To fully understand, one must be willing to give everything—and yet, perhaps, lose nothing at all. The path must be walked, not held at arm's length."

Nour nodded, her gaze distant. "This place wasn't created for those who seek control or glory. It was made to test those who truly seek to understand."

Amal turned back to the mosaic, her mind racing as she examined the tiles. "Each tile is a step in the Phoenix's journey… creation, destruction, rebirth." She touched a tile depicting the bird engulfed in flames. "This… this one represents sacrifice."

Tariq knelt beside her, his voice softer now. "And if we don't get it right?"

Amal looked into his eyes, her own gaze steady. "Then we fail, and the Phoenix remains locked away, beyond anyone's reach."

He swallowed, his voice tight. "And what happens to us?"

She hesitated, the weight of his question sinking into her. "I don't know. But we came here to find the truth, and I can't turn away now."

Tariq sighed, his voice resigned. "Then let's get it right."

They began slowly, moving through the stages depicted on the mosaic, each one revealing a part of the Phoenix's eternal journey. Amal's fingers brushed over tiles of ash and flame, of life springing anew from the embers. With each touch, the room seemed to grow warmer, the air charged with a growing, watchful presence.

Nour's voice broke the silence. "This power… it's waiting for you, Amal. I can feel it. But remember, the Phoenix's gift isn't just about taking. It demands something back."

Amal met her gaze, a flicker of determination crossing her face. "I know. I'm willing to give what it asks."

Tariq clenched his fists, his voice a quiet murmur. "And what if it's more than you're willing to give?"

She looked at him, her face softened by a faint, bittersweet smile. "Then… I trust that you'll know what to do."

The final tile depicted the Phoenix in its full glory, wings spread wide, surrounded by flames. Amal's hand hovered over it, her heartbeat loud in her ears. She glanced back at her companions, seeing the tension and worry in their faces, yet feeling the same conviction she had felt from the very beginning.

She pressed down on the tile.

A sudden surge of heat swept through the room, a roaring inferno of sound and light that swallowed them whole. For a moment, she felt herself dissolving, pulled into the very cycle of creation and destruction, and in that instant, she understood: the Phoenix's power was not just a force—it was a calling, a choice to be part of something far greater, a cycle that transcended any one life.

When the heat faded, they were left standing in silence, the room filled with a new energy, a presence that lingered around them like a silent promise.

Amal's voice was quiet but unwavering. "We've unlocked it. But now... now the true test begins."

Amal's hands trembled, hovering just above the final mosaic tile. Her breath came shallow and fast, her fingers feeling as though they were wrapped in the weight of all the ancient power that coursed through the room. Each heartbeat seemed to pulse in time with the glowing symbols on the floor, as though the temple itself were alive, waiting for her next move.

The genie's voice, calm yet heavy, broke the silence. "Amal," he said, stepping closer, his gaze intense. "Before you go any further, you must understand... awakening the Phoenix is no small act. This isn't a choice you can take back."

She looked up at him, her face pale but her eyes bright with a fierce determination. "I know. I know this isn't something we can undo. But we didn't come here to stop halfway."

The genie's expression remained solemn. "Then you understand that by awakening it, you're choosing to bind yourself to its cycle. You won't just witness the Phoenix—you will be part of it. Its fire will touch everything you are, everything you will become."

Amal took a steadying breath, glancing down at her trembling hands. "I... I feel it already. This weight, like the power's already calling to me. It's terrifying, but... isn't that what we came for? To understand?"

Tariq's voice came from behind, soft yet edged with worry. "Amal, listen to him. Once you do this, there's no guarantee you'll come out the same. Or that you'll come out at all."

She turned to him, her gaze softening. "Tariq, I know you're worried, but… we've faced everything together so far. I've felt this pull since the moment we entered this city. This power—it's part of me now."

He stepped closer, his hands resting on her shoulders, his voice barely above a whisper. "And what about you? What if it takes you, changes you? I can't… I can't lose you to this."

She closed her eyes, feeling the warmth of his hands grounding her, calming the storm inside her for a moment. "I'm still here, Tariq. This is me, just as I've always been. I need you to believe in that."

He exhaled, his gaze darkening. "I want to. But this is bigger than us, Amal. This… it feels like something that doesn't just demand strength—it demands everything."

Nour, who had been watching from the side, spoke up, her tone both somber and strangely reverent. "Tariq's right, in a way. The Phoenix's fire isn't just power; it's purpose. And purpose demands a sacrifice. Amal, if you're willing to take that risk, then I believe you're already part of the cycle."

Amal turned to Nour, her voice steady despite the tremble in her hands. "Then guide me, Nour. Help me understand what it wants from me."

Nour took a step forward, her gaze locking onto Amal's. "It doesn't want just obedience, Amal. The Phoenix seeks something deeper—resolve, conviction. A willingness to let go of who you were to become something… more."

Amal nodded slowly, feeling the words settle over her like a weight and a balm all at once. "Then that's what I'll give it."

The genie's face softened, a flicker of sadness in his eyes. "Amal, once you take this step, you're bound to the Phoenix. Your life will no longer be yours alone."

Amal's voice grew quieter, almost a whisper. "Maybe it never was."

Tariq shook his head, his expression anguished. "Don't say that, Amal. You're more than just a… a vessel for some ancient power. You're my sister, you're—"

"I know, Tariq." She met his gaze, her expression gentle but unyielding. "And that's why I have to do this. If we turn back now, everything we've sacrificed, everything we've endured… it would all be for nothing."

He clenched his jaw, his hand tightening on her shoulder as though he could anchor her there by sheer will. "Then promise me you'll come back. That this power, whatever it is, won't take you from me."

She smiled, a small, sad smile. "I promise, Tariq. I'll come back. But I have to go forward first."

Nour nodded, her voice filled with a solemn respect. "Then speak the words, Amal. Let the Phoenix hear your resolve."

Amal closed her eyes, taking a deep breath as she summoned every fragment of courage within her. Slowly, she began to murmur the incantation Nour had taught her, each word falling from her lips like an ember, catching in the air and lingering before fading. The symbols on the mosaic floor responded, flaring to life beneath her, the heat growing until it felt as though the very ground were made of flame.

As she spoke the final word, the energy surged, and Amal felt a wave of warmth spread through her, washing over every part of her being. She was no longer just Amal; she was part of the Phoenix's story, woven into its cycle of life, death, and rebirth.

The genie's voice came as a final, quiet reminder. "Remember, Amal… this power may seek to consume, but it is your resolve that will control it. Hold to that, or lose everything."

And as the fire of the Phoenix pulsed within her, Amal knew the weight of his words—but even so, her resolve did not falter. She had chosen her path, and she would see it to the end.

The ground beneath them trembled, each tile in the mosaic shifting as if part of a massive, ancient mechanism. Amal's hand still hovered over the final tile, the pulse of energy beneath it intensifying with every passing second. She could feel it—an immense, watchful presence, waiting, as if held in a breath that would be exhaled any moment. Her heart thundered in her chest, the enormity of the moment sinking into her bones.

Tariq's voice broke through, edged with fear. "Amal, something's wrong. We need to stop—whatever you just did, it's... it's waking something."

Amal didn't turn to him, her gaze locked on the shifting patterns beneath their feet. "This is it, Tariq. This is what we came here for." Her voice was quiet but resolute, as if speaking too loudly might shatter the fragile balance holding everything in place.

Tariq took a step back, his instincts screaming at him, filling his veins with cold dread. "And what if it's not what we thought? Amal, we don't know what we're dealing with here—this isn't just a puzzle anymore. It's alive."

Nour moved beside them, her gaze fixed on the mosaic, her voice filled with awe and a hint of reverence. "Alive, yes. The Phoenix has always been more than legend. It's a force, a flame that exists in the world beyond our understanding. Amal's unlocked the first step—there's no stopping it now."

Tariq shook his head, panic edging into his voice. "Then we were wrong to come here. Amal, please, listen to me. You don't have to go through with this. Whatever this is, we can still walk away."

Amal finally looked at him, her face shadowed but her eyes shining with a light that was almost... otherworldly. "Tariq, I can feel it. This power—it's waiting for me. It's like it's been calling to us from the start, leading us here."

He took her hand, his grip firm, a desperate attempt to anchor her. "And if it takes you? If you wake whatever is in here and it consumes you?"

Her fingers tightened around his, her voice softer. "Then I'll know that I faced it. That I didn't run when the moment came." She paused, a bittersweet smile crossing her face. "You always told me I was stubborn."

"This isn't just stubbornness, Amal. This is…" he gestured to the trembling floor, the faint glow that now spread outward from the center of the mosaic, "this is… a force beyond anything we're ready to face. I don't want you to become part of something that demands more than we can give."

The genie's voice interrupted, his tone both calm and grave. "This moment was bound to happen, Tariq. The Phoenix's power has awaited its awakening, and Amal's spirit… her resolve, has been the catalyst. She is part of its cycle now, whether any of us wish it or not."

Tariq turned to the genie, anger and desperation flickering in his eyes. "Then tell me—what happens to her? What does this 'awakening' even mean? Because all I see is my sister risking herself for something we don't even understand."

The genie's face softened, his gaze steady as he addressed Tariq. "It means she steps into a cycle older than time—a power that binds life, death, and rebirth. The Phoenix's flame is both creation and destruction. It will demand everything and leave nothing the same."

Amal's voice was barely a whisper. "I understand the risk, Tariq. But this... this is my choice." She released his hand, stepping forward to face the swirling mosaic as it began to glow brighter, a deep, fiery red. The warmth surged around them, making the very air shimmer with intensity.

Tariq clenched his fists, helplessly watching her. "And what am I supposed to do? Just... watch you disappear into whatever this is?"

She looked back at him, her face softened by a mixture of sadness and determination. "Trust me, Tariq. I'm still here. And I'm doing this not just for me, but for us. For everything we've sacrificed to get here." She placed her hand back on the final tile, feeling the heat rising through her fingertips, an acceptance of the power's call.

Nour's voice was a murmur, half to herself. "The Phoenix... it's awakening."

At those words, the mosaic shifted again, and the room trembled as though responding to a great, silent heartbeat. An intense light burst from the center of the floor, spreading outward like waves, filling the entire chamber with a blinding glow. Amal felt the warmth flooding through her, wrapping around her like a living flame, filling every inch of her being.

Tariq watched in horror, his voice a strangled whisper. "Amal!"

But she was beyond his reach now, her eyes shut, her body surrounded by a ring of fire that spun and danced around her, vibrant and fierce. For a moment, she felt as though she were floating, weightless, her spirit mingling with the flames, merging into the vast power that lay within the Phoenix's essence.

Then, suddenly, the light dimmed, the flames receding until only a faint glow lingered around her. She opened her eyes, and as she looked at her brother, there was a strange light in her gaze—a strength, a knowledge that hadn't been there before.

She smiled softly, a hint of sadness mingling with triumph. "I understand it now, Tariq. The Phoenix… it's not just power. It's… purpose." Her voice was steady, calm, the tremor gone from her hands.

Tariq took a tentative step forward, his eyes searching her face for any sign of the sister he knew. "Are you… are you still you?"

She nodded, a gentle warmth in her smile. "Yes. And I feel… whole. As though everything we've done, everything we've sacrificed, has led me to this moment."

The genie's voice carried a note of quiet reverence. "The Phoenix has accepted her. She is bound to it now, a guardian of its flame."

Tariq's hand finally relaxed, though his gaze remained wary, as if afraid that the sister standing before him was both familiar and somehow changed forever. And as the mosaic continued to pulse beneath their feet, Amal realized that this was only the beginning—the Phoenix had awakened, and with it, a purpose greater than any of them had yet understood awaited her.

Chapter 11
A Rift in Purpose

The air grew colder as Amal and Tariq descended into the depths of the ruins, the shadows thickening around them with each step. The walls were lined with intricate carvings, their meanings hidden in the murky darkness, but even the weight of ancient knowledge didn't dampen the tension simmering between them.

Tariq's footsteps slowed, his expression clouded as he watched Amal press forward, seemingly oblivious to his growing unease. Finally, he couldn't hold back any longer. "Amal, stop. Just… stop."

She paused, looking back at him, her brow furrowing. "What is it? We're almost there—I can feel it."

"That's exactly the problem," he shot back, his voice tight with frustration. "You're so focused on getting there, on finding this 'truth,' that you're not even stopping to think. This place isn't just dangerous—it feels wrong, like it's meant to keep people out. And maybe there's a reason for that."

Amal's eyes flashed, her voice sharp. "And maybe there's a reason we're here. We've come too far to start questioning everything now, Tariq."

He took a step toward her, his tone intensifying. "Questioning everything? Amal, that's what I've been doing since the moment we set foot in this place! But you—you're so obsessed with discovery, with finding whatever secret you think this Phoenix holds, that you're willing to risk both our lives."

Her jaw clenched, her eyes narrowing as she met his gaze. "Do you think I don't know the risks? Do you think I don't feel it every step of the way?"

"Then why can't you stop?" His voice softened, the frustration giving way to a hint of desperation. "Why can't you just... take a moment to realize what's at stake here? This isn't just some academic pursuit, Amal. This is our lives. Your life."

Her voice dropped, intense and unyielding. "Because this matters, Tariq. More than you understand. More than even I fully understand. But I know it's worth it. I didn't spend years preparing, studying, giving up everything else, just to turn back because of fear."

"Fear?" he echoed, incredulous. "You think this is about fear? Amal, this is about survival. This is about not throwing away everything you've worked for, everything we've been through, because you're chasing a myth."

Amal took a sharp breath, her voice tight with controlled anger. "It's not a myth. It's knowledge, it's power, and it's within reach. You of all people should understand that."

"Understand what?" He threw his hands up, exasperated. "That you're willing to die for some ancient story? That your obsession is more important than the people around you?"

She glared at him, her fists clenched at her sides. "This isn't just a story, Tariq. It's a purpose. My purpose. You knew that when you came with me."

Tariq's voice dropped to a harsh whisper, his frustration and fear palpable. "I came with you because I thought I could keep you safe. Because I thought maybe, just maybe, you'd be reasonable. But you're blinded, Amal. Blinded by your ambition."

She recoiled slightly, a flicker of hurt crossing her face, but she didn't back down. "Ambition? You call it ambition, but you don't understand what it means to search for something your entire life, to feel like everything has led you to this point. This isn't just about me."

"Then what is it about?" he demanded. "Because all I see is you, charging forward without any regard for what might happen, for who might be left behind if something goes wrong."

Amal's voice softened, but her gaze was fierce. "It's about meaning, Tariq. About finding something bigger than ourselves. Don't you feel it? This place… it's calling to us. It's calling to me."

Tariq took a deep breath, shaking his head. "I don't feel anything except a pit in my stomach that's only getting worse the deeper we go. And maybe that's because I'm the only one here who realizes how dangerous this really is."

She crossed her arms, her expression defiant. "Then go. If you're so afraid, if you're so convinced this is wrong, then turn back. No one's forcing you to be here."

His face fell, the anger in his eyes giving way to something raw and vulnerable. "I'm here because I care about you, Amal. Because I can't stand the thought of you getting hurt. But every step we take… it feels like I'm watching you slip further away, like you're being pulled into something you don't fully understand."

She looked at him, her gaze softening, the edge of her anger dulling. "Tariq, I know you care. And I care too. But I need to do this. I have to see it through, for me—for everything I've sacrificed."

He let out a shaky breath, glancing away. "And what about us? What happens if this obsession of yours… if it takes you too far?"

She reached out, touching his arm gently, her expression resolute. "Then that's a risk I have to take. And if you're willing to stay with me… then I'll be grateful. But I'm not turning back, Tariq."

He searched her face, the conflict clear in his eyes as he struggled to reconcile his loyalty with his fear. After a long pause, he nodded, his voice barely a whisper. "Alright. But don't expect me to watch quietly while you throw yourself into the fire."

Amal's gaze softened, a faint, almost sad smile crossing her lips. "I wouldn't expect anything less."

They stood in silence, the tension between them thick and unresolved. But for now, it was enough. With a final glance, they turned back to the darkened passage, each step a reminder of the distance—both physical and emotional—that lay between them, yet bound them all the same.

The silence stretched between them, thick with the weight of their unresolved tension. Amal's determined stride slowed, and she glanced back at Tariq, her gaze softening as she saw the exhaustion and worry etched into his face. She paused, her resolve flickering as memories surfaced, memories of a time when the dangers they faced were merely dreams and ideas.

"Tariq," she said quietly, her voice losing its edge. "Do you remember… that summer, when we were kids? The one where we'd camp outside, trying to find constellations and looking for meteors?"

Tariq looked up, surprised by the gentleness in her tone. He gave a slow nod, a faint smile tugging at the corners of his mouth. "Yeah. You'd stay up all night, staring up at the sky, convinced you'd find something new."

Amal chuckled softly, her gaze distant as she recalled those nights under the stars. "I was certain, wasn't I? Convinced I'd discover something no one else had ever seen." She looked at him, her eyes warm. "And you were always there, right beside me. Even when you wanted to go back inside, you stayed."

He shrugged, a bit of the tension melting from his shoulders. "Someone had to keep an eye on you. Make sure you didn't wander off into the woods, looking for imaginary star maps."

She laughed, and the sound was a balm to the strained air between them. "That was the deal, wasn't it? You'd keep me grounded, and I'd keep pulling you into adventures you never asked for."

Tariq sighed, his gaze softening as he studied her face, illuminated by the torchlight. "I remember how much you loved those stories—the legends, the myths. You'd make up your own tales about the stars, connect them to things I'd never even thought about."

"That was where I first heard the story of the Phoenix," Amal murmured, a touch of wonder in her voice. "Sitting out there under the stars, listening to that old storyteller. He talked about rebirth, about resilience… it felt like magic."

Tariq nodded, a bittersweet smile forming. "You were so young. But I think… you understood it more deeply than the rest of us did, even back then."

Amal met his gaze, her eyes searching his face. "You understood it too, Tariq. You did. That's why you were always there with me. We wanted the same things—discovery, purpose… something bigger than ourselves. That's what this is about."

He looked away, his expression conflicted. "Maybe I understood it once. But I didn't expect that dream to bring us here… to something so real, so dangerous."

She stepped closer, her voice gentle. "That's the thing about dreams, Tariq. They start as stories, ideas… but when you chase them far enough, they can become something real. That's what we always wanted, wasn't it? To go beyond the stories, to make those dreams ours?"

He sighed, the last of his resistance melting as he heard the earnestness in her voice. "I suppose so. But somewhere along the way, that dream became yours. And I just… forgot what it was like to believe in something so fully."

Amal placed a hand on his arm, her tone both comforting and resolute. "You never forgot, Tariq. You're still here. You came with me because you believe in it, too. And not just for me—for us. Because this is something we were meant to do together."

He met her gaze, his expression softening with reluctant acceptance. "Maybe you're right. Maybe I just needed to be reminded." He let out a slow breath, his tension dissipating as the memory of their shared past rekindled a familiar warmth.

They stood in silence, the weight of their earlier conflict fading as they reconnected over memories that were older and deeper than their fears. Amal took a step back, smiling softly. "So, are you ready to keep going? To find what we came here for?"

Tariq nodded, a small, resigned smile appearing. "Yeah. Let's see this through. I'd hate for you to get all the glory while I was busy worrying."

Amal laughed, giving his shoulder a light squeeze. "I'd never let you miss out on that. Besides, who else would I share it with?"

Tariq returned her smile, the light in his eyes more hopeful, more certain. "Then let's go," he said, his voice steadier. "We're in this together, for better or worse."

With a renewed sense of purpose, they continued deeper into the ruins, side by side, their footsteps echoing in unison. The path ahead was still shadowed, but together, they felt ready to face whatever lay in the darkness, bound by shared memories and the dream that had brought them this far.

The silence between Amal and Tariq now felt different—not strained, but warm, infused with the memory of shared dreams and rediscovered purpose. They paused at the edge of a dimly lit chamber, shadows flickering around them as they prepared to press on.

Tariq looked at her, his face softened by a newfound clarity. "Amal... I need you to know. I'm not just here because I feel obligated to protect you. I'm here because I believe in what we're doing, in what you're doing. I forgot that for a while, but... not anymore."

Amal's eyes brightened, her gaze meeting his with gratitude and relief. "I'm glad, Tariq. I know I've been pushing hard, maybe too hard. But having you here… it means everything. I never wanted this to be something I had to do alone."

He gave a slight nod, a smile tugging at his lips. "You're not alone. Not in this. I'm with you, fully. Not because of our promises to each other or our family, but because I finally remember why I wanted to be here in the first place."

She took a deep breath, her voice quiet but sincere. "Then let's see it through together. No more second-guessing each other. No more fear."

Tariq let out a low chuckle, raising an eyebrow. "No more fear? Amal, we're headed toward something that could be more powerful than anything we've imagined. Fear might be a little difficult to let go of."

She laughed, her shoulders relaxing as she shook her head. "Alright, maybe that's asking a bit much. But no more fear of each other. No more doubting our reasons."

He met her gaze, nodding slowly. "Agreed. No more doubting." He took a deep breath, his voice growing quieter. "Look, I'll admit, I don't know if I'll ever fully understand the pull you feel toward all of this—the Phoenix, the ruins, the symbols. But I don't need to understand it completely to support you. That's what matters, right?"

Her smile was soft, appreciative. "Yes. That's all I could ever ask for. Just knowing that you're with me, that you're... really with me."

"I am," he replied, his tone unwavering. "And whatever comes, I'll be here. Not as your protector, not as some reluctant partner. But as someone who wants to see this dream come true as much as you do."

Amal looked at him, the flicker of a deeper warmth passing through her expression. "Thank you, Tariq. Truly. I... I didn't realize how much I needed to hear that."

Tariq shrugged, a hint of his usual humor returning. "You've always been the one with the words. I'm just the one stubborn enough to stick around." He paused, his gaze growing serious again. "But this time, it's not just about being stubborn. It's about knowing that I'm where I need to be."

She reached out, taking his hand for a brief moment, her grip firm but gentle. "Then let's go forward together. No more hesitations."

He squeezed her hand back, his voice low but resolute. "Together."

They released each other's hands, but the moment lingered, the renewed bond between them palpable. With a final, shared look of understanding, they turned toward the passage that lay ahead. Tariq's face remained cautious, but there was a steadiness in his steps that hadn't been there before.

As they moved forward, Tariq glanced over, his voice almost a whisper. "Just promise me… if things start to feel too dangerous, we'll talk about it. Together."

Amal nodded, her expression open and honest. "I promise. No more going forward without each other."

They shared a smile, their tension now tempered by trust. With renewed purpose, they stepped deeper into the shadows, knowing that whatever they faced, they would face it side by side.

Chapter 12
Reflections of Resilience

The desert seemed to exhale, the winds settling into a calm that was rare in such a barren land. A deep, pulsing energy radiated outward from the heart of the ancient temple, sinking into the sands, flowing like a river through stone and soil. Amal stood at the temple's threshold, her senses alive with the slow, rhythmic beat of power, almost like a heart beginning to stir after a long sleep. It wasn't the raging inferno she had braced herself for, but something subtler, something that hummed with intent and control.

Tariq joined her, his movements careful, his face still pale from the battle but his eyes filled with wonder as he gazed out over the desert. "Is it... supposed to feel like this?" he asked, his voice quiet, hesitant. "I thought the Phoenix's awakening would be... louder, more destructive."

Amal shook her head slowly, her gaze fixed on the horizon as she took in the subtle shifts in the landscape. "I don't know, Tariq. Maybe... maybe the Phoenix's power isn't what we thought it was. It's like..." She trailed off, struggling to find the words. "It's like it's reaching out, touching everything. But there's... restraint."

The genie appeared beside them, his expression solemn as he observed the pulsing magic spreading across the land. "The Phoenix is both life and death, Amal. It is renewal as much as it is destruction. What you feel now is its healing power, the life force it carries."

Tariq glanced at him, a flicker of unease in his eyes. "But that restraint—how long does it last? What happens if it decides it wants more than just... healing?"

The genie's gaze darkened, his tone calm but laced with a hint of warning. "The Phoenix's power is bound by its purpose. So long as it is guided by one with resolve and understanding, it will remain balanced. But without that guidance..." He looked at Amal, his expression grave. "It can turn as easily to ruin as it does to life."

Amal took a deep breath, feeling the weight of his words settle over her. "So, it's on me, then. I'm... responsible for this." She closed her eyes, feeling the pulse of the Phoenix's magic resonate within her. "I can feel it, but it's... hard to hold onto, like trying to carry water in my hands."

Tariq placed a hand on her shoulder, his voice gentle. "Then let me help. You don't have to carry this alone, Amal."

She opened her eyes, a faint smile breaking through her worry. "Thanks, Tariq. I think... I think the Phoenix can sense that too. It's responding to our connection, to our purpose." She looked down, the glow in her eyes flickering with a hint of uncertainty. "But there's something... deeper. It's almost like... like it's testing me."

Tariq's grip on her shoulder tightened. "Then don't let it push you past your limit. We've already come so far—don't let this thing take more than it has to."

The genie nodded slowly, his gaze distant. "The Phoenix's spirit will ask for everything, but it will not take unless you allow it. You are bound to its fire, yes, but that fire can be controlled if you remain true to your purpose."

Amal glanced back at him, searching his face for reassurance. "And if I lose control?"

His eyes softened, a rare warmth breaking through his usual reserve. "Then you will have those around you who will remind you of who you are. The Phoenix chose you for a reason, Amal. Trust in that, and it will trust in you."

The desert around them shifted, patches of barren land springing to life as the Phoenix's magic coursed through the sand, turning it a lush green in places, while nearby, rock formations glowed with an otherworldly energy, cracks and fissures healing before their eyes. Tariq's face lit with awe as he watched the transformation.

"It's... beautiful," he murmured, almost to himself. "I've never seen anything like this." He looked over at Amal, his expression filled with pride. "You're doing this, Amal. You're guiding the Phoenix."

But she shook her head, her voice quiet but filled with worry. "No... it's the Phoenix guiding me. I don't know where it'll take us, or what it might ask of us next. This... this isn't a gift without a price, Tariq. I can feel it."

He nodded, his face sobering. "Then whatever it asks, we face it together. You said it yourself—we didn't come this far to let fear stop us."

She took his hand, her resolve growing, though a flicker of doubt remained in her eyes. "Then let's hope we're ready for whatever it brings. Because I don't think it's done testing us yet."

And as the magic continued to pulse across the desert, spreading like veins of fire through the earth, Amal knew that this was only the beginning—the Phoenix had awakened, and with it, a future neither of them could yet see.

As the desert pulsed with new life around her, Amal felt a strange, disquieting calm settle over the landscape. Everywhere she looked, green sprouted from the once-barren sands, flowers unfolding in vibrant colors, their petals stretching toward the sky as if they had always belonged to this forgotten land. And yet, in the center of all this life, a stillness lingered deep within her—a quiet emptiness that left her uneasy.

Tariq approached her, his gaze sweeping across the transformed desert. "It's... incredible. Look at it, Amal. You've brought life back to a place that was nothing but dust and rock."

She nodded, her lips pressed into a thin line. "It feels like a dream," she whispered, glancing down at her hands, still warm from the Phoenix's energy. "But something… it's strange, Tariq. It doesn't feel… complete."

He frowned, studying her face. "What do you mean? Isn't this the Phoenix's power? The land's healing, the magic's flowing through everything—"

She cut him off, her voice tinged with uncertainty. "No. This… this isn't everything. It's as if I've only released a fragment of its power. The Phoenix… it's still waiting." She placed a hand over her heart, where she could feel a faint, pulsing warmth, like a candle that hadn't fully caught fire. "It's almost like I only… unlocked the door."

Tariq's eyes widened, realization dawning on him. "You mean… this isn't the full awakening?"

She shook her head, frustration flickering across her face. "I thought I had completed the ritual. The symbols, the incantation, the mosaic—it all seemed to lead to this moment. But there's a depth to the Phoenix's power that I haven't reached yet." She looked out over the desert, watching the landscape as it came to life in waves, the vibrant greens stretching out as far as she could see. "It's like the Phoenix gave me a piece of itself. But the true power… it's still dormant, still waiting."

The genie stepped forward, his expression thoughtful, his eyes taking in the revived landscape with something akin to reverence. "The Phoenix's nature is layered, Amal. It does not awaken all at once. What you've felt, what you've released, is only the beginning. The Phoenix will rise when it is fully ready, and that readiness depends as much on you as it does on the ritual."

Her brow furrowed, her voice carrying a hint of frustration. "But I don't understand. If this is only a fragment… then what was all of this for? What did I awaken if not the Phoenix itself?"

The genie's gaze softened, his tone calm and patient. "The Phoenix has many forms, many stages of rebirth. Each fragment is a promise of what it can become, and what it can offer. You've released its essence—the power of creation, of renewal. But the spirit of the Phoenix, its full consciousness, still lies dormant. It is testing the world, testing you."

Amal let out a slow breath, feeling the weight of his words settle over her. "So, it's not finished. And that means this peace… it's temporary."

Tariq shook his head, his voice laced with disbelief. "After everything, after nearly losing ourselves… we've only just started?"

The genie nodded, his voice solemn. "You have set events in motion, Amal, but the Phoenix is bound by a cycle. It will awaken fully only when all conditions are met—when the world is ready for its fire. And until then, its magic will test, it will heal, and it will wait."

Amal looked out over the blooming desert, a flicker of sadness in her eyes as she watched the delicate blossoms opening, fragile against the vastness of the sands. "Then this is a glimpse... a promise of what could be, but not a guarantee. We've only delayed the inevitable."

Tariq's expression darkened. "So what are we supposed to do now? We've risked everything, and yet we're no closer to truly understanding this power. Are we just supposed to wait? Watch as it... teases us with pieces of itself?"

The genie's face softened, his tone almost gentle. "Patience is part of the Phoenix's test, Tariq. This is not a power to be taken lightly or rushed. You've felt its light, seen its touch upon the land. But only those who honor the Phoenix's full journey will know its true awakening."

Amal nodded, her voice filled with quiet resolve. "Then I'll wait. I'll do what it takes to be ready when the time comes." She looked at Tariq, her eyes determined. "This isn't over, Tariq. We may have to wait, but we're still part of this."

Tariq sighed, nodding slowly. "I know. I just... after everything, I thought we'd have reached an end. That there'd be some kind of closure."

She offered him a small, reassuring smile. "Maybe we will, one day. But for now... we know we've done something right." She gestured to the green, the vibrant life around them. "This, at least, is real."

The three of them stood in silence, watching the desert as it blossomed under the Phoenix's influence, a reminder of both their progress and the journey that still lay ahead. And as the magic pulsed gently beneath the surface, Amal felt the

Phoenix's presence—patient, waiting, an unbroken promise of what was still to come.

The desert lay in quiet aftermath, the vibrant green of newly awakened life a stark contrast against the desolate sands stretching beyond. Scattered remnants of the battle littered the ground, symbols of the cost of their journey. The Ashen Veil had withdrawn, their dark cloaks barely visible on the distant horizon as they retreated, battered but still resolute, a threat diminished yet lingering like a shadow over the landscape.

Amal stood at the temple's threshold, her gaze fixed on the faint figures disappearing into the sands. Her heart was heavy, each breath carrying a mixture of relief and the weight of decisions yet to come. She turned, catching Tariq's watchful eyes on her, a complex mixture of emotions swimming in his gaze.

"Is it over?" he asked, his voice quiet yet thick with weariness.

Amal looked away, her fingers tracing patterns in the dust. "The Veil has retreated, but... this doesn't feel like an end, Tariq. It feels like a pause. The Phoenix... it's not finished. Not yet."

Tariq's expression darkened. "So we risked everything, nearly lost each other, and for what? A fragment of a power that won't even let us rest?" He shook his head, a note of frustration creeping into his tone. "What's the point if there's no real end to this?"

She winced at the bitterness in his voice. "It's not that simple. The Phoenix isn't just a single moment of power or a weapon to wield. It's… alive, Tariq. We've only unlocked a fraction of what it can do because that's all it's ready to give. And maybe…" She hesitated, her voice softening, "maybe that's all we're ready to receive."

He crossed his arms, his gaze skeptical. "And you're okay with that? Just accepting whatever scraps of power it decides to give us? You were so sure, so certain that this was worth it… but look at what it's cost us, Amal. Was it?"

Her face fell, uncertainty flickering in her eyes as she struggled to find the words. "I don't know. I thought I was ready for this. For whatever it meant to awaken something so ancient, so… powerful. But standing here now, after everything… I don't know what it means for us anymore."

Tariq's voice softened, a trace of pain seeping through. "Then why didn't you listen to me? Why couldn't you see the risk before we lost everything?"

Amal looked down, guilt weighing heavily in her eyes. "Because I didn't want to believe that the Phoenix's power could come with such a cost. I thought… I thought it would be worth it, that if we just reached it, everything would fall into place." She paused, glancing at the blooming desert around them. "But I see it now. This power… it's unpredictable. It doesn't answer to us; we answer to it."

Tariq sighed, running a hand over his face. "So what happens now? We wait, and hope that this fragment of the Phoenix doesn't decide it wants more?"

She met his gaze, the gravity of their situation settling between them. "Yes. I think that's all we can do—learn from it, guide it if we can. Maybe there's more we're meant to understand before it fully awakens."

He shook his head, the tension finally easing into a weary resignation. "I just don't know if I can keep going like this, Amal. Constantly wondering what's next, if this power is going to take something more from us."

She reached out, placing a hand on his arm, her voice steady but filled with a sadness that matched his. "I know. And if you need to step away from this, I'll understand. You didn't ask for this journey, Tariq. You followed me because you trusted me."

He looked at her, something unreadable in his eyes. "And I still do, Amal. But I also need to know that this trust isn't going to lead us down a path we can't survive."

She nodded, the unspoken weight of his words echoing in her heart. "Then maybe… maybe we learn to live with what we've started. To find peace, even if it's temporary, with the power we've released. And if the Phoenix stirs again… we face it together, just like we always have."

A faint smile tugged at his lips, bittersweet yet accepting. "Together, then." He looked out at the desert one last time, the green stretching before them like a reminder of both their success and the price they'd paid. "But promise me, Amal… no more secrets. If we keep going, we're in this together. No more hiding anything."

She swallowed, guilt flashing in her eyes before she nodded. "No more secrets, Tariq. I promise."

As they stood side by side, watching the desert in its fragile new state, Amal felt a quiet understanding settle between them—a shared acceptance of the unknown that lay ahead. They had come seeking power, but what they found was something far more delicate: a fragile peace, as fleeting and powerful as the Phoenix's flame itself. And as long as they held onto each other, she felt that perhaps they could endure whatever the future brought.

Chapter 13
Scorched Histories

The chamber was vast, its walls stretching upward to a ceiling lost in shadows. Faded torches flickered against the rough stone, illuminating patches of a mural that dominated the far wall. Intricate and haunting, the mural's colors were worn but unmistakably vibrant, depicting scenes of fire, loss, and rebirth in rich, sweeping strokes.

Amal moved toward it, her fingers hovering near the ancient art, her eyes wide with awe. The mural was a story frozen in stone, a testament to a past both glorious and tragic. Each image flowed into the next, capturing the rise and fall of a civilization, its triumphs and its ultimate downfall.

"Tariq," she whispered, her voice filled with reverence. "Look at this… it's a history. The history of those who sought the Phoenix."

He stepped closer, peering over her shoulder at the swirling images. His gaze landed on scenes of scorched earth and ruined buildings, shadowed figures fleeing from torrents of flame that seemed almost alive. He shuddered. "Is it just me, or does this look like… destruction? Like something meant to be a warning?"

Amal's eyes traced over the mural, lingering on an image of a figure reaching out toward a massive bird enveloped in flame, its wings spreading wide, engulfing everything in its path. But to her, there was a beauty in the devastation, a purpose behind the fire. "Yes… but it's more than that. It's not just destruction. It's transformation."

Tariq's brow furrowed as he took in the mural, his voice thick with concern. "Transformation? Amal, this doesn't look like any kind of rebirth. It looks like they were… consumed. Like they paid some enormous price."

Amal's gaze was intense, captivated as she pointed to another section where a city lay in ruins, figures kneeling before the Phoenix as it hovered above them, flames licking its wings. "They sought the Phoenix's power. They wanted control over something they didn't understand, and they suffered for it. But look—there's reverence here. The Phoenix wasn't just a force of destruction. It offered something, something worth seeking."

Tariq shook his head, his face pale as he looked between the images and her. "But at what cost, Amal? Look at these faces, these people… they look desperate, terrified. They didn't get what they sought. They were left with ruins, ashes."

Amal's fingers traced the outline of the Phoenix, her gaze distant, contemplative. "Maybe they were unprepared. They approached the Phoenix with the wrong intentions, driven by greed, maybe even arrogance. But that doesn't mean the Phoenix is purely destructive. It's a force beyond simple human ambition, something that reshapes and renews, yes, but also requires humility."

Tariq's voice was laced with frustration as he replied. "But who's to say we're any different? What makes you think that we'd be spared from the same fate if we seek this... power? This thing destroyed an entire civilization, Amal."

She turned to him, her expression unwavering. "But don't you see? That's the point. The Phoenix isn't just about power. It's about understanding our limits, knowing when to let go, when to accept transformation instead of trying to control it. The ones who failed wanted the Phoenix's power for themselves. They weren't seeking knowledge; they were seeking dominion."

He let out a harsh breath, his gaze returning to the mural. "And you think we can just... walk in and understand it? Avoid the mistakes they made?"

Amal's eyes softened, and for a moment, her voice was quieter, more reflective. "I think that if we approach the Phoenix with the respect it demands, with the understanding that it's not ours to possess but something to learn from, maybe... just maybe, we'll find what we're looking for."

Tariq was silent, his gaze tracing the mural, the haunting images of devastation and sacrifice etched deep into his mind. He watched her as she continued studying the Phoenix, a figure of both beauty and terror. To him, the mural screamed of ruin, a warning carved into stone, but in her eyes, he saw something different—a sense of purpose, of reverence that almost frightened him.

"What if we're wrong?" he murmured, his voice barely audible. "What if we're not... worthy of this knowledge? What if it consumes us too?"

Amal turned to him, placing a hand on his arm, her gaze steady. "Then we go forward together, understanding that every step we take has meaning. We're not seeking to control it, Tariq. We're here to learn, to understand. That's the difference. That's why we're different."

He looked at her, his expression conflicted but softened by her certainty. "I just don't want to see you end up like... them." He gestured at the mural, his voice raw with emotion. "These people... they gave everything. And for what?"

"For something they believed was greater than themselves," she replied quietly, her gaze returning to the mural. "And maybe they failed. But we can learn from them. We have to believe that, Tariq. Otherwise, what's the point of any of this?"

Tariq sighed, nodding reluctantly. He looked at the mural one last time, taking in the dark, haunting images of the past. He still couldn't shake the fear gnawing at him, the sense that they were stepping into something they might not fully understand. But Amal's conviction, the unwavering resolve in her eyes, stirred something within him.

"All right," he said, his voice steady but cautious. "We keep going. But if this starts to feel... wrong, if it looks like we're heading toward the same path as them... we stop. Promise me that."

Amal met his gaze, a small, determined smile touching her lips. "I promise. We'll be careful, Tariq. We're not here to make the same mistakes. We're here to learn from them."

With one last look at the mural, they turned back to the path ahead, their footsteps echoing softly against the cold stone floor. The haunting images remained behind them, but the weight of the past hung over them, a reminder of the delicate line between discovery and destruction.

As they moved deeper into the chamber, shadows danced along the walls, illuminated by their torchlight, casting flickering shapes over the faded murals. The images of fire and ruin seemed to pulse with life, a silent testament to the Phoenix's power. Tariq's face was tense, his gaze flicking uneasily over the charred scenes and the figures captured in desperate moments. Meanwhile, Amal's eyes gleamed, filled with a determination that, to him, seemed almost reckless.

"Amal," Tariq began, his voice low but edged with urgency. "You saw what those people went through—the ruins, the scorched earth. How can you still think of this as anything other than a threat?"

Amal stopped, turning to face him, her expression resolute. "Because that's not all it is, Tariq. The Phoenix is more than just a force of destruction. It's rebirth, it's transformation. Yes, there's danger, but there's also potential—potential that can't be ignored."

He shook his head, frustration tightening his jaw. "Potential? Amal, we're looking at an ancient civilization that was wiped out. They sought the Phoenix, and look what happened to them. You really think we're different?"

"I think we have a choice in how we approach it," she replied, her tone calm but unyielding. "They didn't understand what they were dealing with. They were blinded by greed, by the desire to control something they couldn't comprehend. But we're not here to control the Phoenix. We're here to learn from it."

Tariq crossed his arms, glancing back at the haunting images on the wall. "And you don't think that's exactly what they thought, too? Maybe they didn't start with the goal of control, but look where they ended up. They were swallowed by it. Devoured."

Amal took a breath, her gaze softening as she watched him. "Tariq, I get that you're afraid. But I believe that this isn't just about us. The Phoenix is... it's a force that's existed for centuries, maybe longer. It's part of something larger than any one of us, and I think it's meant to challenge us."

"To challenge us?" He echoed, incredulous. "Do you even hear yourself? This isn't some test we can ace and get through without consequences. This isn't a 'challenge'—it's a threat."

She sighed, turning away slightly as if choosing her words carefully. "Maybe it's both. Maybe it is a threat, but one with purpose. Like a wildfire that clears a forest for new growth. The

Phoenix doesn't destroy for the sake of destruction; it does so to make way for something new."

He shook his head, his frustration simmering beneath the surface. "Amal, that sounds like a pretty justification for something you don't fully understand. You think you can just shape the Phoenix to your vision of renewal and hope, but what if it's not interested in being 'understood'? What if it's just… fire?"

She looked at him, a flicker of pain in her eyes, but she didn't back down. "And what if we're meant to be the ones to bring that understanding? What if we're here to find a way to harness it, to make it something that can help instead of destroy?"

Tariq exhaled, running a hand through his hair as he glanced at the mural again. "I'm not saying we shouldn't seek answers. But maybe we don't need to get as close as you're trying to. We can study the Phoenix, understand its power without… invoking it, or whatever it is you're imagining."

Amal's eyes narrowed slightly, her voice dropping. "That's where you and I differ, Tariq. I don't believe in standing at the edge of something powerful and hoping it reveals itself from a distance. If we're going to find any answers, we need to face it. Fully."

He hesitated, his gaze searching her face. "You really believe that, don't you?"

"Yes," she replied firmly. "I do. I think that, unlike those who came before, we have the chance to approach the Phoenix with respect. I believe it can be more than just destruction, that it has something to offer if we're willing to see beyond the danger."

Tariq sighed, a trace of sorrow entering his voice. "I just hope that by the time you realize the danger… it's not too late."

For a moment, they held each other's gaze, a silent understanding passing between them, a mixture of shared history and starkly different visions of the path ahead. Amal's resolve didn't waver, her conviction clear and unshakable. Tariq, however, felt a gnawing sense of unease, a dread that no words could dissipate.

"Then let's go," she finally said, her voice soft but firm. "But know that I'll see this through, Tariq. Whatever the cost."

He nodded reluctantly, his gaze lingering on the mural one last time. "Then I'll be there, watching out for you. Even if I don't share your faith in… whatever this is."

They turned back to the path ahead, each carrying a different burden—Amal's an unyielding determination, and Tariq's a quiet, persistent fear. Yet together, they pressed forward, bound by a shared purpose, though the gap between their beliefs seemed wider than ever.

The flickering light from Amal's torch cast wavering shadows across the ancient mural, giving life to the faces frozen in anguish and awe, to the symbols etched as warnings or perhaps as desperate pleas for understanding. Amal's gaze was fixed, absorbing the images and the silent, haunting story they told. Where others might see doom, she saw potential—a path that had been abandoned, misunderstood, and feared. But that wouldn't be her story. She would find a way forward, one that honored the Phoenix without succumbing to the mistakes of the past.

Tariq watched her in silence, his heart heavy with conflicting emotions. Her fascination, her drive—they were things he had always admired. But here, in the dim light of a forgotten ruin filled with foreboding, those same qualities took on a darker hue. He felt a pulse of dread, a warning echoing through his mind, as if the Phoenix itself was reaching across time to caution him. The very walls seemed to murmur, whispering of flames and failure.

"Amal," he said, his voice steady but tinged with an edge of caution. "You're really set on going forward, aren't you?"

She nodded, her gaze unwavering. "This isn't just about what happened here in the past, Tariq. It's about what's possible now. They might have failed, but we don't have to repeat their mistakes. I can feel it… like the answers are right there, just out of reach."

Tariq took a slow breath, glancing between her and the images of destruction scrawled across the wall. "But what if those answers come with consequences? You saw what happened here—this isn't just some forgotten ruin. People paid a price for reaching too far."

Amal turned to face him, her eyes alight with conviction. "I know. And I don't dismiss that. But the Phoenix… it's not just some chaotic force. I think it's misunderstood, misinterpreted. Power like that—it's not inherently destructive. It's about how we approach it."

Her voice softened, an almost pleading tone slipping in. "Tariq, I know you're worried. And I don't blame you. But think about what we could accomplish if we find the answers they couldn't. We could bring back something the world has forgotten, something that could transform everything."

He met her gaze, feeling the weight of her determination pressing down on him. Her words tugged at memories, at the spark they'd shared as children, dreaming of unearthing secrets hidden by time. But the reality of their journey had turned those dreams into something else, something that left a pit of worry settled deep within him.

"Amal… I don't know if I believe in this the way you do," he said, his tone laced with regret. "But I do know I can't let you face it alone. If you're set on this… if you're really, truly set… then I'll stay by your side. Just promise me you'll keep an open mind, that you'll recognize the risks for what they are."

She smiled, gratitude softening the intensity in her eyes. "I promise. I'm not going into this blindly, Tariq. And I wouldn't ask you to follow me if I thought this was hopeless. I just… need you to trust that this path has a purpose. That it's worth it."

A long silence hung between them, thick with unspoken doubts and hopes. Despite every instinct screaming at him to pull her back, to insist they turn around, he found himself nodding. He couldn't abandon her—not here, not after everything they'd faced together. And if anyone could find a way to navigate the Phoenix's trials without succumbing to the fate of those who'd come before, it was Amal.

"Then let's go," he said, the quiet resignation in his voice softened by the strength of his resolve. "But remember, Amal... I'm with you. Every step. But if things start to feel beyond control, we stop. Together."

Her gaze was steady as she looked at him, her smile tinged with relief. "Thank you, Tariq. I don't take that promise lightly. Whatever comes, we'll face it. Together."

With a final shared glance, they turned toward the passage ahead, the shadows stretching out before them like the unknown future. The path was laden with warnings and memories of ruin, yet they walked forward with the assurance that no matter what they found, they would meet it side by side.

Chapter 14
Awakening the Fire

The desert stretched before them, transformed in ways that felt almost miraculous. Where once there had been only lifeless sand and barren rock, streams now glistened, weaving their way through the landscape like veins of silver under the early light. Verdant patches of green sprouted along the banks of these new rivers, clusters of wildflowers and grasses that bent in the gentle breeze. Trees, saplings now, dotted the landscape, and as the trio moved further into the desert, the scent of fresh earth mingled with the lingering warmth of the Phoenix's magic.

Amal stood at the edge of one of these rivers, her expression a mixture of wonder and unease as she knelt to touch the cool, clear water. It trickled through her fingers, as real as any river she had ever seen, yet its origins were rooted in magic far older and wilder than anything she fully understood.

"This was once nothing but sand," she whispered, half to herself. She glanced over at the genie, her brow furrowing. "This is... more than I expected. More than I thought possible."

The genie stepped forward, his gaze drifting over the landscape with a somber appreciation. "The Phoenix is not just fire, Amal. It is the life born of flame, the regrowth that follows devastation. What you see here is only the beginning of its influence."

Tariq, his arms crossed, watched the growing landscape with a cautious eye. "But what happens when it decides it's given enough life? Will it just… leave all this to wither, or is this its permanent gift?"

The genie shook his head, his voice calm but thoughtful. "The Phoenix's gifts are as unpredictable as they are profound. It is a cycle—creation and destruction in equal measure. What it gives, it can just as easily take away if it senses imbalance."

Amal's gaze lingered on the delicate blooms unfurling along the riverbank. "So, it's fragile. This life… it feels so solid, but it's built on magic that could vanish as quickly as it came." She looked up at the genie, her voice soft but firm. "Then how do we protect it? How do we make sure that this isn't just a fleeting vision?"

The genie turned to her, his expression unreadable. "You don't, Amal. Not entirely. Magic like this is not meant to be held or controlled. It responds to need, to purpose. If you wish for this life to last, you must guide it, nurture it… but not attempt to bind it."

Tariq let out a breath, a wry smile tugging at his lips. "So, in other words, we're supposed to just hope it all stays as it is? That doesn't exactly feel… secure."

"No," the genie agreed, a hint of amusement in his gaze. "It isn't secure. The Phoenix's flame does not allow for certainty. But perhaps, in embracing that uncertainty, you'll find a way to protect what it has given."

Amal stood, looking out over the river winding its way into the desert, new life clinging to its edges. "So, we stay vigilant," she said, more to herself than anyone else. "We guide what we can, make sure it doesn't spiral into something destructive."

Tariq gave a short nod, glancing at the genie. "And if it does start to shift? If the Phoenix decides to turn all this life to ash one day?"

The genie's expression softened, a shadow of understanding passing over his face. "Then you face it, as you would any force of nature. You don't command it, but you respect it, respond to it. And with that respect, you may be able to shape its impact."

Amal's eyes drifted back to the blossoming desert, her voice quiet. "So this world… this world that the Phoenix is remaking… it's not permanent. It's a gift with a price."

"Exactly," the genie said, his voice both a warning and a reassurance. "The Phoenix's power is bound to the cycle, and so long as you understand that balance, it will respond to you. But if greed, fear, or the desire for control enters that balance…" His voice trailed off, the unspoken threat lingering in the air.

Tariq glanced at his sister, his gaze steady. "Then we make sure it never comes to that. We protect this—this world, this change. Not because we own it, but because we're part of it."

Amal smiled, the tension easing from her face. "Yes. We don't own it… we just have the privilege of watching over it." She placed her hand over her heart, feeling the faint, steady pulse of the Phoenix's magic within her, a reminder of the power that had made all of this possible.

The genie nodded, a faint but genuine smile crossing his face. "Then let this be your new beginning, Amal, Tariq. Guard it well, and perhaps the Phoenix will see fit to keep its flame in balance, granting life where once there was only desolation."

And as they stood by the river, watching the first tendrils of green reach for the light, they felt, perhaps for the first time, a fragile but real hope that the Phoenix's gift was not merely an illusion, but a chance to build something enduring from the ashes.

Iskar limped through the barren stretch of desert, his dark cloak trailing behind him like a shadow, heavy with dust and blood. The few remaining members of the Ashen Veil followed at a distance, their faces set in grim silence, their expressions unreadable as they absorbed the sting of their defeat. Each step was a reminder of the battle, of the power that had turned against them in ways they had not anticipated. Iskar's gaze burned with a fierce determination despite his injuries, his hand clenched tightly around a dark staff.

One of his men stepped forward, hesitant, his voice a whisper. "Iskar... perhaps we should consider another approach. This... this magic is beyond even what we were prepared for. Perhaps—"

Iskar's voice, cold and unyielding, cut through the quiet. "Perhaps nothing. The Phoenix's power is dangerous, yes, but it is also powerful beyond measure. Do you truly believe we should walk away from that? Surrender because we were… outmatched?" His tone dripped with disdain, his eyes narrowing as he surveyed his followers.

The man hesitated, lowering his gaze. "No, sir. But the girl… she commands the Phoenix now. We can't simply take that power without facing her again. And the genie… he's not bound anymore. He's dangerous."

Iskar's face twisted in irritation, his words laced with bitterness. "Yes, I am quite aware of the genie's newfound freedom. That was a miscalculation on our part." His gaze drifted toward the temple, barely visible on the distant horizon. "But nothing is without weakness. Even the Phoenix, with all its glory and power, can be subdued. Its spirit is bound to that girl, and I assure you… everyone breaks, given the right pressure."

One of the others stepped forward, her voice quiet but filled with a simmering resentment. "Iskar, what if we're wrong? What if trying to contain this power only leads to more loss? We've already lost so many."

Iskar's eyes flashed, his expression growing colder. "Then those losses were necessary sacrifices. The Ashen Veil has existed to protect this world from the Phoenix's destruction, even if it costs lives. If we abandon our mission now, then we dishonor everything we've fought for."

The woman held his gaze, her voice steeling. "But at what cost? The Phoenix's power is bound to her by choice, by destiny. We may be fighting against something that isn't meant to be contained."

Iskar's jaw clenched, his voice turning to a low, menacing growl. "Are you questioning our purpose, Lara? Do you doubt the centuries of vigilance we've kept? Do you truly believe that a single girl and her misguided ideals will save this world from the Phoenix's flames?"

Lara's face tightened, but she met his gaze, defiance flickering in her eyes. "I don't know. But I know that what I saw in that temple was not just power—it was balance, a purpose beyond simple control. She's not trying to wield it like a weapon, Iskar. She's protecting it. Maybe… maybe we need to rethink our approach."

Iskar's hand tightened on his staff, his voice icy. "Then you're free to leave if your conviction falters so easily." He turned his back on her, his eyes fixed on the temple in the distance, his voice a soft but unbreakable vow. "But I will not rest until the Phoenix is contained. That power… it will consume her in time. All I need to do is wait until the fire takes more than she can handle. And when it does, I will be ready."

The man from earlier shifted uncomfortably, glancing between Iskar and the other members of the Veil. "And what if you're wrong, Iskar? What if she learns to control it?"

Iskar's lips curled into a bitter smile. "Control? You think she can control a force as ancient and volatile as the Phoenix? No one commands it—not her, not the genie, not anyone. She is a spark, and one day she will burn out, leaving only ashes. We simply need to ensure that when she falls, we're there to seize what remains."

Lara's voice, softer but no less firm, broke the tense silence. "And if she doesn't fall? If she becomes something stronger, something... untouchable?"

Iskar's smile faded, his gaze hardening. "Then we break her before she can. And if she resists, then we make her pay the price for standing in our way." He turned to the rest of his followers, his eyes narrowing with dark resolve. "Prepare yourselves. We may have retreated today, but this isn't over. The Phoenix will awaken in full, and when it does, we will be there to claim its flame."

The others nodded, some with a shadow of reluctance, others with renewed determination. The desert stretched out before them, a wasteland marked by the scars of their failed conquest. But Iskar's expression held no remorse, only a fierce, unwavering commitment to the path he had chosen. He could feel the weight of their mission, the burden of the Ashen Veil's purpose pressing down on him like iron.

As they began their slow, weary march across the sands, he muttered under his breath, more to himself than to anyone else. "This is not over. The Phoenix may rise, but it will be bound by us, or it will be destroyed."

And with those words, he led his fractured order back into the endless sands, carrying with him a determination that was both fearsome and chilling, a promise that the Ashen Veil would return—stronger, unrelenting, and more dangerous than ever. The battle had been lost, but the war, he knew, had only just begun.

Amal sat beside the river that had formed overnight, watching as the water twisted and shimmered under the morning sun. The delicate greenery that had emerged along its banks seemed fragile, its roots just beginning to take hold in the shifting sands. She felt a strange, grounding calm as she watched life continue to unfurl, each leaf a quiet testament to the power she and her brother had unleashed. Beside her, Tariq was silent, his gaze as fixed and contemplative as her own.

"Do you think it'll last?" he finally asked, his voice soft, hesitant. "All of this… the life, the magic. It feels so… temporary."

Amal glanced at him, her expression unreadable. "Maybe it is," she murmured, her voice distant, thoughtful. "But I think that's part of the Phoenix's nature. It creates, and it destroys, but it doesn't do either forever. What it leaves behind… it's up to us to protect it, nurture it." She hesitated, then added, "We're part of this, Tariq. Whether it lasts or not depends on what we do now."

He turned to face her fully, a hint of incredulity in his eyes. "So you think this—" he gestured to the blossoming desert, the life slowly unfolding around them, "this is our responsibility now? After everything we've done… you still want more of this?"

Amal's gaze didn't waver. "It's not about wanting it, Tariq. It's about what we've started. The Phoenix's power isn't something we can just unleash and walk away from. It's going to change things, and not just here. The Veil will come back for it; others will try to understand it, maybe even try to claim it. If we leave now, we'd be leaving it unguarded."

He sighed, rubbing a hand over his face. "But we've barely made it this far. What if we're in over our heads? What if we can't handle what's coming?"

Amal smiled, though there was a shadow of worry in her eyes. "Maybe we are, but… I think that's part of the journey. We weren't meant to understand everything all at once. It's like the Phoenix itself—layers we have to uncover, lessons we have to learn as we go. We're only at the beginning, Tariq."

He looked away, his gaze drifting back to the river, his face etched with an intensity that she knew masked both fear and resolve. "So, what, we just… keep going? Keep searching for more pieces of this? More mysteries that could either save or destroy everything?"

She placed a hand on his shoulder, her voice gentle but firm. "Yes. Because if we don't, then we leave those mysteries to people like Iskar, people who don't see the balance, only the power. We've seen what the Phoenix can do, and we know it's more than just fire or destruction. But if we walk away… that's all it'll ever be."

Tariq let out a long breath, a reluctant smile tugging at his lips. "You make it sound so simple, like it's just another step forward. But this… this feels huge, Amal. Bigger than anything we've done."

She nodded, her own smile bittersweet. "It is. But we don't have to face it alone. We have each other, the genie… and whoever else we might find along the way. We're building something, something bigger than ourselves. Doesn't that feel… right?"

He chuckled softly, shaking his head. "You really are impossible, you know that? No matter what, you always find a way to turn it into something worth doing."

Amal's smile grew, her eyes gleaming with a fierce determination. "Maybe that's just what we're meant for. Maybe we're meant to see things others can't, to take risks they won't." She paused, looking out at the distant horizon, where the desert met the sky. "There's a whole world out there, Tariq. A world filled with secrets, with hidden magic. We've only begun to scratch the surface."

He nodded slowly, the resignation fading from his face, replaced by a cautious hope. "Then I guess we have our mission. We keep going, keep searching, keep guarding what we can. For as long as it takes."

She held his gaze, her expression one of quiet resolve. "For as long as it takes."

The genie approached them then, his expression one of calm understanding. "You've made your choice," he said, a note of respect in his voice. "To carry the Phoenix's flame is a path that few would dare take, and yet you have chosen it willingly."

Amal looked up at him, her voice steady. "We've chosen it because we believe it's worth protecting. This world, its magic… it's fragile, and there's so much we don't understand. But we're ready to learn."

The genie inclined his head, a rare smile softening his features. "Then I am honored to continue this journey with you. Together, we will face whatever lies ahead, and in doing so, perhaps we will bring more than just survival to this world. Perhaps we will bring balance."

Amal and Tariq shared a look, a silent agreement passing between them. And as they turned their backs on the river and set their sights on the distant horizon, they felt a new purpose guiding them, a purpose that burned brighter than any doubt, stronger than any fear.

The world awaited, filled with secrets and power, both ancient and yet undiscovered. And with each step, they knew that the journey they had begun, the path they had chosen, would shape not only their lives but the future of magic itself.

Chapter 15
The Heart of the Phoenix

The narrow passage opened into a vast, shadowed chamber. Flickers of light emanated from the edges of the room, casting long, spectral shadows that played over the ancient stone. At the far end, a massive doorway loomed—arched and imposing, it seemed almost to pulse with a life of its own, as though guarding the power that lay beyond. Amal took a steadying breath, her eyes set with determination. But as they stepped forward, a familiar, cloaked figure emerged from the shadows.

The genie's gaze was as intense as ever, his dark eyes fixed on them with a gravity that seemed to make the air grow colder. He stood silently for a moment, barring their way with an authority that was both calm and immovable. "You have reached the final threshold," he said, his voice low and resonant, each word carrying the weight of ancient warnings. "Beyond this doorway lies the heart of the Phoenix. Once you cross, there is no turning back."

Tariq felt a chill run down his spine, the genie's words striking a chord of fear he could no longer suppress. He glanced at Amal, his voice tense. "Amal, maybe... maybe we should stop here. We've come so far. We don't know what awaits us beyond that door. This isn't a simple discovery. This... this could change everything."

Amal didn't waver, her gaze locked on the doorway, her face set with fierce resolve. "That's exactly why we can't turn back now, Tariq. This is what we came for. This is what we've been searching for our entire lives."

The genie's expression softened, but his tone remained grave. "You misunderstand what lies beyond, seeker. The Phoenix is not a prize to be won, nor a secret to simply uncover. Its power will alter you in ways you cannot yet fathom. It is the force of rebirth itself, but it demands a price."

Tariq's hand tightened on Amal's arm, his voice barely a whisper. "Did you hear him, Amal? This isn't just about gaining knowledge. He's telling us that we might not come back the same... if we come back at all."

Amal met Tariq's gaze, her eyes unwavering. "I hear him. But I didn't come this far to be afraid of what lies ahead. The Phoenix is about change, transformation. We can't seek it without accepting that it may change us, too."

The genie stepped closer, his voice dropping to a solemn whisper. "There is a difference, seeker, between change and loss. The Phoenix does not merely grant power; it reveals the deepest truths of one's soul. Once those truths are laid bare, there is no going back to who you once were."

Amal swallowed, a flicker of doubt crossing her face, but it was quickly replaced by the fierce glint of determination. "I understand the risks. I'm willing to face them. This is bigger than us, bigger than fear."

Tariq turned to her, his face pale, his voice shaking. "Amal, please. We don't have to do this. We've uncovered so much already. We could turn back now, return with everything we've found. Isn't that enough?"

She looked at him, her expression softening slightly, a hint of sadness flickering in her eyes. "Tariq, I know you're afraid. And maybe I should be, too. But this... this is my calling. If I turn back now, I'll live the rest of my life wondering what could have been, what truths we left behind."

The genie's gaze shifted between them, his expression inscrutable. "Your resolve is admirable, seeker. But know this: beyond that door lies a path that only the true of heart and the unwavering of purpose can walk. Many have reached this threshold, and few have returned unchanged... if they returned at all."

Tariq clenched his fists, his voice pleading. "Amal, just think for a moment. This isn't just about you. You have people who care about you, who would be devastated if... if you didn't come back."

Amal placed a hand on his shoulder, her touch both firm and gentle. "And that's why I have to go, Tariq. For everyone who believes in me, everyone who has supported me. I have to see this through, for them and for myself."

The genie inclined his head slightly, acknowledging her determination. "Very well, seeker. If you choose to proceed, know that the Phoenix will test you in ways you cannot anticipate. It will reveal every strength... and every weakness."

Amal nodded, her voice steady. "Then I'm ready. I'll face whatever lies ahead."

Tariq's face was etched with worry, but he gave a resigned nod, his voice quiet. "Then I'm with you. No matter what happens, I won't let you face this alone."

With a final look at the genie, Amal turned toward the towering doorway, her steps resolute. The genie watched them both, his gaze unreadable as he stepped back into the shadows, leaving them with one final, solemn warning echoing through the chamber:

"May your hearts be as steady as your resolve, seekers. For beyond this door lies the fire that will either forge or consume you."

As they crossed the threshold, the weight of his words settled heavily on their shoulders, but together, they took the first step into the unknown.

As Amal and Tariq stepped through the towering doorway, a surge of energy met them, thick and electric, making the air feel alive. The chamber seemed to hum, its walls covered in symbols that pulsed with a faint, rhythmic glow, almost as if the stone itself were breathing. The atmosphere was charged, both ominous and magnetic, drawing them deeper into the heart of the Phoenix's domain.

Amal's eyes widened, taking in the raw, uncontained power emanating from every surface. "This... this is it, Tariq. We're in the Phoenix's chamber."

He swallowed hard, his gaze darting around, tension tightening every muscle. "I can feel it, Amal. It's like... it's watching us, like it's aware we're here."

She looked over at him, her expression softened by understanding but resolute. "I know you're scared, Tariq. I am, too. But this is why we came. This is what we've been searching for."

Tariq took a steadying breath, his voice low, almost pleading. "Amal, are you absolutely sure about this? This place... it feels alive, but not in a way that makes me feel welcome. It feels... like it's testing us already."

Amal nodded, her gaze unyielding as she met his eyes. "I feel it too. But we've made it this far, and there's no turning back now. We both knew there would come a point where we'd have to commit completely. This is that point."

He looked down, clenching his fists as he struggled with the weight of his decision. "And if... if something goes wrong, Amal? If this power is more than we can handle?"

She reached out, placing a hand on his arm, her voice gentle but steady. "Then we face it together. Whatever happens in this chamber, we're here because we believe in something bigger than fear."

He exhaled, his expression torn between dread and loyalty. "I don't want to lose you to this… this force we can barely understand. Amal, I don't know if I can handle that."

She squeezed his arm, her tone reassuring. "You won't lose me, Tariq. I'm here, fully aware of the risks. And I trust that whatever happens, we'll come out of this stronger."

He searched her face, desperation flickering in his eyes. "But this isn't just about trust or belief, Amal. This place is… it's beyond anything we've prepared for. It feels like it's pushing us to see if we'll break."

Amal's gaze didn't waver. "And maybe that's part of it. Maybe the Phoenix's power is meant to push us, to see if we can withstand it, to see if we're worthy. This isn't a challenge for the faint-hearted."

Tariq let out a shaky breath, his voice barely above a whisper. "What if… what if I'm not as strong as you? What if I'm the one who can't handle it?"

She took his hand, her voice soft but fierce. "You are strong, Tariq. You've come this far, despite every doubt, every fear. And that's exactly why you're the person I wanted by my side. We balance each other."

A brief silence settled between them, heavy with unspoken fears and mutual resolve. Finally, Tariq nodded, his grip on her hand tightening. "Then let's keep going. I won't let you do this alone."

They shared a final, intense look, one filled with understanding and an unbreakable bond. Amal released his hand, but the connection between them felt stronger than ever as they turned to face the heart of the chamber.

With a deep breath, Tariq spoke, his voice steadier now. "No matter what happens… I'm here. We cross this line together."

Amal nodded, her gaze fixed on the pulsing light ahead. "Together," she whispered, taking the first step forward, with Tariq right beside her, both prepared to face whatever lay beyond.

Amal stepped toward the pedestal at the center of the chamber, her heart racing with anticipation. The pedestal was carved from dark stone, its surface covered in intricate symbols that seemed to shimmer faintly under the torchlight. As she placed her hand on the cold stone, a low rumble began to echo through the chamber, vibrating up through her fingers and into her chest.

The ground beneath them shook, and the walls came alive, symbols lighting up in a brilliant cascade, pulsing with a rhythm that felt like a heartbeat—ancient, powerful, unstoppable. An intense light filled the room, streaming from the walls and pooling around the pedestal, casting everything in a blinding, golden glow.

"Amal… what did you just do?" Tariq's voice trembled, his eyes wide with fear as he instinctively took a step back.

Amal didn't move, her hand still on the pedestal, her gaze fixed on the light gathering before them. "I think… I think we've awakened it. This is the Phoenix."

The light swirled, forming a vortex above the pedestal. Flames sparked to life, twisting and spiraling into the shape of an enormous bird, its wings spanning the width of the chamber, feathers flickering and shimmering like molten gold. Its eyes opened, two blazing orbs that seemed to pierce straight into their souls.

Tariq gasped, stumbling back as the heat washed over him, intense and suffocating. "Amal, this… this isn't right. It's too powerful! We shouldn't be here!"

Amal stood transfixed, her face illuminated by the golden light, her eyes wide with awe. "This is exactly where we need to be, Tariq. Look at it. This is the Phoenix. The heart of everything we've been searching for."

The Phoenix turned its gaze toward them, its eyes narrowing, as if measuring their worth. A deep, resonant hum filled the chamber, a sound that seemed to echo both within and outside of their minds, like the voice of something ancient and unfathomable.

Tariq's voice shook, barely a whisper. "Amal… it's looking at us. It's… it's alive."

"Yes," she breathed, unable to look away. "Alive, and aware. We've woken something greater than ourselves, something… extraordinary."

"Extraordinary?" Tariq's voice rose in desperation. "This is more than extraordinary, Amal. This is terrifying. We don't know what it wants, what it's capable of!"

Amal turned to him, her expression fierce and resolute. "And that's why we're here—to find out. To understand. Don't you see? This is our chance to be a part of something bigger than ourselves, to touch something no one else has ever touched."

Tariq shook his head, his voice tight with fear. "But at what cost, Amal? Just being here feels… it feels like we're standing at the edge of something that could destroy us."

The Phoenix let out a low, rumbling cry, flames rippling across its form, filling the room with a heat so intense that it felt as if the air itself might ignite. Tariq shielded his face, the sheer force of the heat pushing him back.

"Amal, please," he pleaded, his voice cracking. "Step back. We don't know what it's going to do."

But Amal held her ground, her gaze locked on the Phoenix, her voice steady and filled with a reverence that bordered on defiance. "If we back down now, we'll never know, Tariq. This is why we're here. This is why I'm here. I won't let fear hold us back."

The Phoenix's gaze shifted between them, its fiery eyes lingering on Amal with a mixture of curiosity and approval, before turning to Tariq, its gaze colder, more critical. He felt its eyes bore into him, as if it were weighing his fear, his hesitation.

Tariq's heart pounded, every instinct screaming for him to flee, but Amal's presence kept him grounded. He looked at her, her face illuminated by the Phoenix's light, her expression serene, fearless. "Amal… are you really ready to face this? To accept whatever it brings?"

She nodded, her voice unwavering. "Yes, Tariq. I am. I believe the Phoenix has a purpose, a reason for choosing us. We just have to be brave enough to meet it."

The Phoenix let out another resonant call, its voice filling the chamber, reverberating through the stone and through their bones. Tariq felt the sound in his chest, heavy and daunting, yet a part of him—some small, stubborn part—began to understand Amal's conviction. This was a power beyond human understanding, a force that demanded respect and courage.

Taking a deep, trembling breath, Tariq steadied himself. He reached out, his hand finding hers, his voice barely above a whisper. "If you're going to face this… then I'll be by your side. No matter what happens."

Amal squeezed his hand, a faint smile crossing her lips as they stood together, facing the awe-inspiring and terrifying power of the Phoenix. She looked up at the fiery bird, her voice filled with determination. "We're here. And we're ready."

The Phoenix regarded them both, flames swirling in its eyes, as if deciding the fate of these two mortals who dared to stand before it.

Epilogue
Ashes and Embers

The desert stretched out in all directions, golden sands shimmering under the soft light of dawn. The winds had finally calmed, leaving only a faint whisper that seemed to echo the events of the night before. Amal and Tariq stood at the edge of the ancient city's ruins, gazing at the remnants of the journey that had forever altered them.

Amal's face was marked with a strange blend of exhaustion and contentment, as though she had uncovered the world's greatest secrets and found peace in their mystery. She turned to Tariq, her expression softened by the first light of morning. "We did it," she whispered, a sense of wonder lacing her voice.

Tariq nodded, still trying to comprehend all they had seen and learned. The chamber's powerful energy, the Phoenix's radiant form, the feeling of standing in the presence of something beyond human understanding—it lingered in his memory, an indelible mark. "I still can't believe we came out of it," he replied, his voice carrying a mixture of awe and disbelief. "That we're here, after everything."

They both remained silent for a moment, watching as the sun rose, casting long shadows over the ruins that had held the Phoenix's secrets for so long. The genie, their silent observer, had vanished when they exited the chamber, leaving them alone to face the aftermath of their journey. His last words echoed in Tariq's mind: *"The Phoenix offers truth, but it also demands sacrifice."*

Amal's thoughts mirrored his own, though she was less burdened by the genie's warning. Instead, she was filled with a quiet satisfaction, knowing they had gone further than anyone else. "Do you feel it?" she asked, her gaze still fixed on the horizon. "That energy, that... presence. It's like a part of the Phoenix remains with us."

Tariq looked at her, a faint smile tugging at the corners of his lips. "It's hard to ignore, especially after seeing the Phoenix up close. But it doesn't feel quite the way I thought it would. It's more... grounding."

Amal nodded, her face thoughtful. "Maybe that's the real power of the Phoenix. It doesn't just consume—it renews. It's not about gaining power over the world, but understanding how to live in balance with it."

They both fell quiet, reflecting on the journey that had brought them here, the trials they had faced, and the Phoenix's final blessing—an understanding that was less about power and more about wisdom. They had glimpsed something beyond the mortal realm, and though it had left them changed, it had also grounded them in a profound way.

After a while, Tariq broke the silence. "What now?" he asked, his voice soft.

Amal turned to him, a glint of excitement sparking in her eyes despite her fatigue. "Now, we take this knowledge back. We share it, not as some grand secret, but as a lesson for those who are willing to listen. Maybe we're not meant to reveal everything, but what we've learned… it could guide others."

Tariq chuckled, shaking his head. "I don't think everyone is ready for tales of ancient cities and firebirds. They'd say we've been out in the desert too long."

"Maybe," she replied with a smile. "But some will understand. And for those who are willing, this knowledge could help them find their own path." She paused, her expression turning serious. "The Phoenix's power is a reminder of what happens when we seek too much, push too far without considering the cost. It's a warning as much as it is a gift."

They began walking back toward the distant edge of the desert, their footsteps quiet as the sun climbed higher, warming the sands beneath their feet. Tariq's thoughts drifted to the memory of the genie's cryptic words and the figures depicted in the murals—the seekers who had come before, who had tried to claim the Phoenix's power and paid the price. A part of him still wondered if they had been lucky, if their escape from the chamber was due to their intent or something far beyond their control.

"Do you think the Phoenix… approved of us?" he asked, glancing at Amal.

She considered the question, her eyes contemplative. "I think it allowed us to leave because we didn't try to take its power. We respected it, didn't try to possess it. Maybe that's all it wanted—to be seen for what it is, not as a tool but as a force, a being in its own right."

Tariq nodded, a sense of relief washing over him. "So, no grand treasure, no hidden powers—just… understanding."

Amal smiled, a peacefulness in her expression that he hadn't seen before. "Yes. And I think that's enough."

As they continued on, the weight of their journey began to settle in—a mixture of exhaustion, revelation, and an odd sense of fulfillment. They had not uncovered a secret weapon, nor had they gained any power to change the world overnight. Instead, they had returned with something quieter, something that couldn't be quantified or wielded. It was a deeper understanding of the world, and of themselves, and the knowledge that they were part of a cycle far greater than their own lives.

In the distance, the faint outline of their camp appeared, and they could make out figures waiting for them—friends and family who had worried, who had questioned the purpose of their journey. Tariq felt a rush of anticipation mingled with trepidation. How would they explain all they had seen? How could they convey the Phoenix's lesson without sounding like madmen?

But Amal seemed at ease. She glanced at him, her face bright with confidence. "We tell them the truth. We share what we've learned, and we trust that those who are meant to understand, will."

He took a deep breath, nodding. For the first time since their journey began, he felt a sense of closure. They had ventured into the heart of an ancient mystery, had stood in the presence of a power that defied comprehension, and had returned with their hearts intact, their souls forever marked by the experience.

As they approached their camp, the desert behind them seemed to fade into a distant memory, yet it remained a part of them, woven into their beings like the sand in their clothes, the warmth of the Phoenix's light in their hearts.

And somewhere, hidden within the depths of the ancient ruins, the Phoenix watched them depart, its flame flickering softly, a silent guardian of secrets that would remain beyond human reach for generations to come.